Contents

Contents

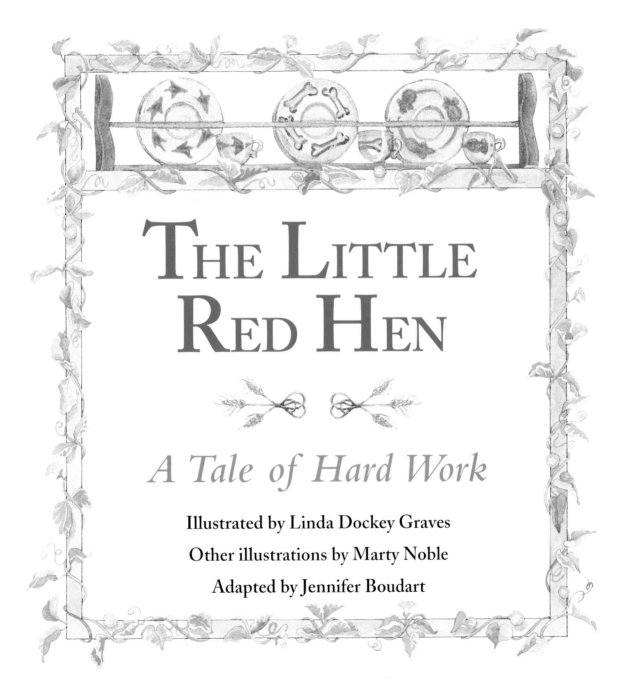

THE LITTLE RED HEN

A Tale of Hard Work

Illustrated by Linda Dockey Graves

Other illustrations by Marty Noble

Adapted by Jennifer Boudart

The little red hen lived next to the road by the farmer's house. Where she lived wasn't very fancy, but she loved it. She shared her home with her five baby chicks and her friends, the dog, the cat, and the duck.

The little red hen worked very hard. She kept the house and the yard neat and clean. There always seemed to be plenty of work to do in order to keep everything looking good.

Everyone liked having a clean house and good food on the table. When it came time to do the chores, though, the others always seemed to have something else to do. As soon as the hen would send her baby chicks out to play, the older animals always seemed to disappear, too. The little red hen did all the work herself. Her days were filled with making beds, cleaning, gardening, and cooking.

One day, the little red hen was sweeping her yard. When she looked down on the ground, she found some kernels of wheat. She put the kernels into her pocket for safe keeping. Then she went to look for the dog, cat, and duck. She found them by the pond. She showed them the kernels and asked, "Who will help me plant these?"

Her three friends looked at each other. Then they looked at the little red hen. "Not us," they said. "Right now we need to take a nap."

"I'll plant them myself," she told them. The little red hen returned to the garden and began digging. Soon her baby chicks came to see what she was doing. They told her they wanted to help. The little red hen and her five baby chicks pretended they were burying treasure. The game made the work go quickly. Soon they had planted all the kernels.

The little red hen visited the garden every day to watch the wheat grow. She made sure the young plants got plenty of sunshine and care.

One day she found her three friends leaning against the farmer's barn. The little red hen said, "There are weeds that are stopping the wheat from growing. Will you help me pull the weeds?"

"I can't," said the cat. "They're all dirty. Do you have any idea how long it takes me to wash my paws?"

The dog and the duck both had excuses, too. No one could help. "I'll just do it myself," said the little red hen. Then she walked back to the garden. Once again, her chicks joined her. They had a contest to see who could pull the most weeds. It was such fun that they finished in no time.

A dry spell kept the rain away for a week. The little red hen was worried about the wheat. If the plants didn't get some water soon, the tender stalks would wither and die. The only thing to do was bring water to the plants. She went looking for her friends. She found them on top of the hay pile. The hen looked up and said, "The summer heat is too strong for the wheat. Who will help me water the garden?"

The dog, the cat, and the duck looked at her. "We're busy writing a song and can't be bothered now," growled the dog. "Didn't you hear me playing my banjo?"

"I'll just water it myself," she said. The little red hen took her watering pail to the garden. Her chicks came to keep her company. The hen pretended to be a thundercloud and tried to sprinkle them with water. Before long, the whole garden had been watered.

The summer sun was very good, and the wheat grew fast. The little red hen and her chicks visited the garden every day. They lovingly tended to the wheat, and it grew strong and hardy. There was going to be a bumper crop!

Soon it was fall and the wheat turned golden brown. The little red hen knew what that meant. She found her friends playing cards under the farmer's wagon. The hen knelt down and said, "Who will help me harvest the wheat?"

The dog, the cat, and the duck kept their eyes on their cards. "Not us!" they mumbled. "Can't you see we're busy?"

The hen stood up and fixed her apron. "I'll harvest it myself," she said. The little red hen took her cutting tools to the garden. This time the five chicks were waiting for her. The family cut the wheat and tied it into bundles. They sang songs, and soon the hard work was done.

Even though she had already spent a great deal of time and energy on the garden, the little red hen knew the work was not finished. She often told her chicks that if a job was worth doing, it was worth doing well.

The little red hen went looking for her friends. She found them sitting by the road. "I need to have the wheat ground into flour," she said. "Who will help me carry it to the miller?"

The dog, the cat, and the duck looked way down the road. The miller was located several miles away. "Not us!" the trio said together. "It's too far for us to walk."

Once again, the little red hen would have to do it herself. She and her chicks left right away. They had a long journey ahead of them, and the chicks moved slowly. The trip seemed to go much faster when they pretended to be hobos traveling with their knapsacks across the country.

The little red hen returned home. She and the chicks were so tired that they soon fell asleep. That night everyone slept very well. The next morning, the little red hen went outside. Her friends were sunbathing on the roof. She called to them, "Who will help me bake bread with my flour?"

The dog, the cat, and the duck didn't even bother looking down. "It's a beautiful day. Who would want to be indoors baking bread?" observed the dog.

The hen shook her head. She thought, "Who would want to spend all day doing nothing?" She told the three, "I'll bake it myself." The little red hen went inside. Her chicks tried to make the bread dough for her. Flour was all over the floor and the chicks, too. They shaped the dough into a big loaf and pretended to be sculptors making a statue. Everyone was sorry to have to stop when the loaf was finished.

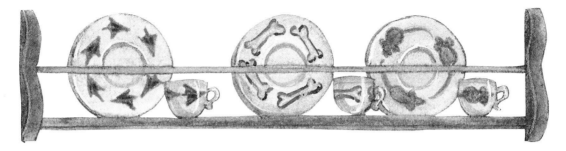

The smell of baking bread floated in the air. The dog, the cat, and the duck came and looked into the kitchen. Two baby chicks danced around the little red hen. She asked, "Who will help me eat this tasty, fresh bread?"

"We will!" squeaked all five of her chicks.

"We will!" cried the group in the doorway.

"Well," said the little red hen, "anyone who helped make this bread can have some. So, if you helped plant the wheat, water it, weed it, harvest it, take it to the miller, or bake the bread, raise your hand!" That night, six tummies got their fill of bread as a reward for work well done.

One to Grow On

Hard Work

Playing is always more fun than working… or is it? Think about how the dog, the cat, and the duck in this story spent their days. Now think about how the little red hen and her chicks spent their days. Who do you think had more fun and excitement?

This story shows us that when you work together, you can have fun, too. You also get to enjoy the rewards of your work. What would you rather spend your time doing?

THE ELVES AND THE SHOEMAKER

A Tale of Hard Work

Illustrated by Kristen Goeters

Adapted by Jennifer Boudart

There once was a shoemaker who lived with his wife. He enjoyed his work very much and set up his shop inside their small house. Times were hard for the shoemaker and his wife. Snowstorms had kept everyone indoors for weeks, so no one could buy any shoes. The shoemaker had little money for food, and he had only enough leather left to make one more pair of shoes. His wife asked, "What are we to do? The cupboards are bare, and we have no firewood. Even our last candle has almost burned away." Her voice was gentle. She knew her husband worked hard for what little they had.

"We must not worry," said the shoemaker. "Things will work out for us. You'll see, I will finish these shoes tomorrow, and someone will buy them." He cut out the leather and then went to bed. The shoemaker would finish working first thing in the morning.

When the shoemaker woke up early the next morning, the whole house was cold. His body shivered, and he was very tired. The shoemaker went to his workbench rubbing his tired eyes. When he looked down, the shoemaker thought he would find the pieces of leather just as he had left them. What he saw instead made him rub his eyes again. A finished pair of shoes were on the workbench!

The shoemaker ran his hands over the shoes. Sure enough, they were made from the same leather that he had cut the previous night. The shoes were very beautiful! The shoemaker admired the tight, even stitching, the placement of the bows, and the silky shine of the leather. He could not have made better shoes himself. The shoemaker called for his wife to come and look at the wonderful shoes. She was just as amazed as he was. "Who could have made these shoes?" she asked.

The shoemaker and his wife did not know who had given them such a wonderful gift. They did know that the shoes were worth a lot and would bring a good price. "What a great day," said the shoemaker. "We have a pair of shoes to sell, and the weather is finally clear. Maybe our good luck will continue and someone will buy these shoes."

At that moment there was a knock on the door. It was a traveler who had seen the shoemaker's sign. "I work for the king," he explained, "and I have been traveling throughout the countryside. My travels have worn holes in my shoes. I was hoping that I could buy a pair from you." The traveler tried on the new shoes, and they fit his feet perfectly. He walked around the shop for a few moments and said, "These are the most  comfortable shoes I've ever worn." Then he gave the shoemaker a shiny gold coin to pay for them.

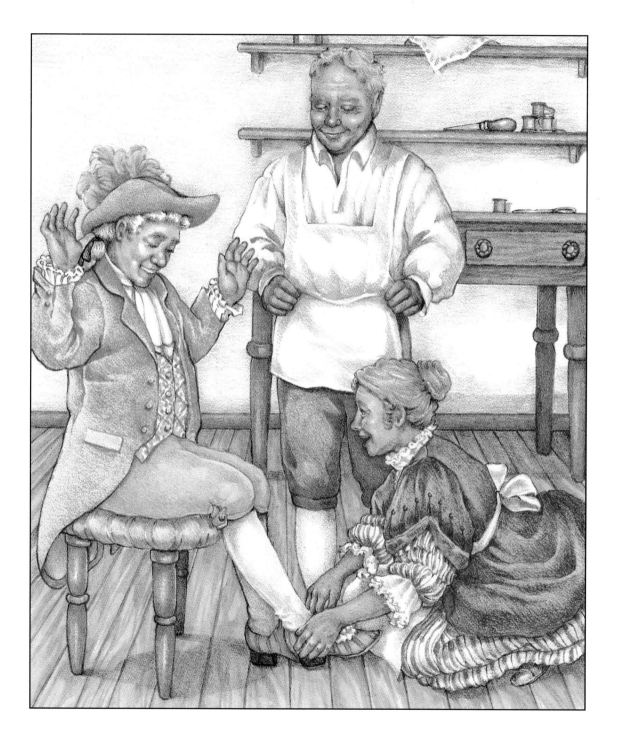

With the gold coin the shoemaker had enough money to buy some things he really needed. He bought food, firewood, and enough leather to make two pairs of shoes. He also bought a wool shawl for his wife.

The couple was very thankful for their good luck, and they decided they would work harder than ever to keep it. Once again the shoemaker cut the leather into pieces ready for sewing and placed them on his workbench. The next morning he found two more pairs of finished shoes. And they were just as good as the first pair!

Within hours the shoemaker sold both pairs of shoes and bought more leather. The next day there were four pairs of shoes waiting on the workbench. This continued for many nights, until the shoemaker's shelves were filled with beautiful shoes like no one had ever seen before.

Life soon changed for the shoemaker. Now he and his wife always had wood for the fire and enough food to eat. The shoemaker bought better tools, lots of leather, and the best brass buckles. He bought his wife an oil lamp, a new blanket, and a lace cap. The shoemaker was always kind to the people who traveled from all over the kingdom to buy his shoes. He could have charged high prices, but instead he charged just enough to live a comfortable life.

Word of the shoemaker's fine shoes made him the most popular shoemaker in the land. He was very happy that his small shop was always filled with people, but still something bothered the shoemaker. One evening he said to his wife, "Every night, while we are tucked in our beds, someone is working hard to help us. It's a shame we don't even know who it is. Why don't we stay up to find out?"

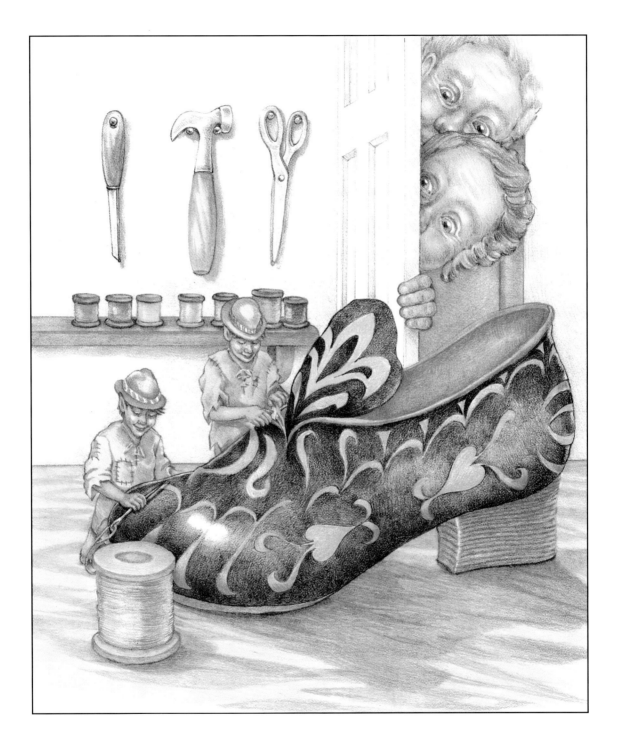

That night the shoemaker cut the leather into pieces and placed them on his workbench. Just like always, he turned down the oil lamp and left the room. But instead of going to bed, he and his wife hid in the doorway.

The moon rose and filled the room with silver light. Soon something was moving on the workbench. Two elves were there! They stood just a few inches tall, no taller than the shoe they were sewing. The elves began to work, helping each other handle the leather and tools. Their clothing was old and worn, which made the shoemaker and his wife sad. The elves wore thin, torn pants and shirts that were ripped and covered with patches. They were making shoes, but they didn't have any for themselves. They must have been cold, but their cheery faces and busy hands didn't show it. The couple tiptoed off to bed, leaving the elves to do their work.

The next morning the shoemaker and his wife looked at the newly made shoes that were on the workbench, and they thought about the elves. "Did you see how quickly those little fellows worked together and how carefully they placed each stitch?" asked the shoemaker.

His wife frowned and answered, "I only saw their poor clothing and bare feet. Clearly they are in great need, yet they work all night to help us."

Her husband agreed and said, "I have an idea! We will make those little elves the clothes they need! They are so tiny that it will be easy for me to make some fine shoes for them."

His wife clapped her hands. "Yes! And I will use a bit of my wool shawl and a corner from our blanket to make proper pants and coats." The couple started right away to make the two tiny suits of clothing.

The shoemaker and his wife finished making the outfits for the elves. That evening, instead of leaving pieces of leather on the bench, they left the clothes and shoes. Once again they hid behind the doorway and waited for the elves to come.

The elves appeared at midnight. They climbed upon the workbench then stopped in their tracks. What was this? Where were the pieces of leather and the tools? The elves were amazed when they saw the clothes. At once they put on the fine new suits. They were so excited they began to sing:

What merry little elves are we!
These fine clothes fit us perfectly!
Who'd be so kind? We wish we knew!
We'd like to give our thanks to you!

The shoemaker and his wife were so pleased they could hardly keep themselves from cheering!

Weeks passed, and the shoemaker's shop was always filled with people. He still offered the finest shoes in the land, and people from all around wanted a pair. He and his wife were very comfortable.

One thing had changed, though. The elves had not come back since the night they received their new suits of clothes. The shoemaker and his wife did not mind. The shoemaker enjoyed his work and was happy to be back at his workbench. He and his wife were glad that they could help the elves who had worked so hard and had been so nice to them.

In the evenings, while the shoemaker cut leather at his bench and his wife baked bread, they thought about the two elves. Because of their kindness and hard work the shoemaker and his wife lived happily. Their cupboards were always filled, and their house was always warm.

One to Grow On

Hard Work

Hard work is the secret to making dreams and wishes come true. This story shows that good things come from working hard. The shoemaker and his wife worked hard, and they were rewarded by the elves coming to help them out. In return the shoemaker and his wife gave the elves the wonderful new clothes. They were grateful to the elves and wanted to thank them for all of their hard work.

We all have different dreams. The shoemaker and his wife dreamed of living comfortably, the elves dreamed of some fine new clothes. No matter what your dream is, hard work can help make it happen.

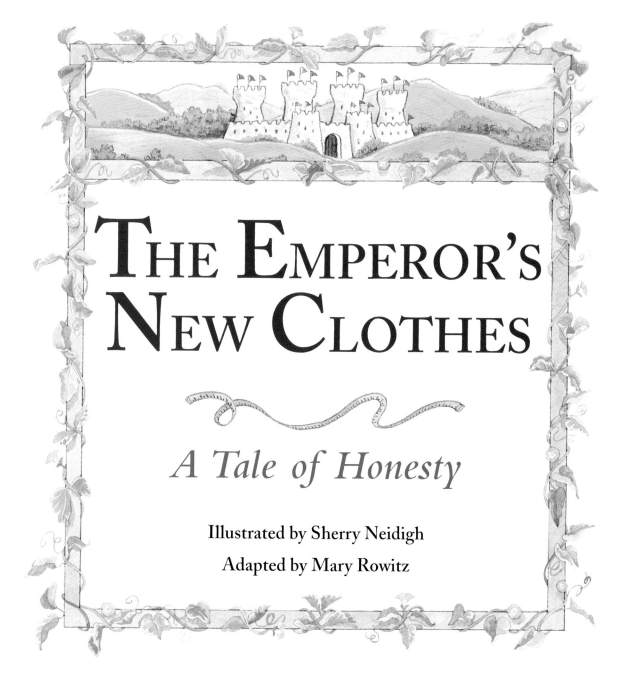

THE EMPEROR'S NEW CLOTHES

A Tale of Honesty

Illustrated by Sherry Neidigh

Adapted by Mary Rowitz

Once upon a time there was an emperor who loved clothes more than anything else. He had more clothes than anyone in the land. The emperor's clothes filled all the closets and most of the rooms in the royal palace.

It was a good thing the emperor was very rich, because he spent so much money on clothes. The emperor selected only the finest, most comfortable fabrics, and he hired the best tailors to work for him.

The emperor also spent a lot of money on mirrors. He thought his fancy clothes made him look quite dashing, so he spent most of his free time looking at himself.

The emperor's pride was well-known throughout the kingdom. Everyone thought he was quite silly to spend so much time in front of his mirrors. They made jokes behind the emperor's back, but no one ever said anything directly to his face. They did not want to make the emperor angry because he was, after all, the ruler of the land.

Word of the silly emperor who loved fine clothes reached two thieves in a faraway land. Instead of making jokes about him, the thieves thought of a way that they could use the emperor's pride to make themselves rich.

The thieves dressed up as traveling tailors and made the long journey to the emperor's palace. They told the palace guards that they had the most wonderful fabric in all of the world, and they asked for permission to show it to the emperor. Of course, the guards let them into the palace.

The sneaky thieves presented themselves to the emperor and his wife. They explained that their fabric was not only wonderful, but magical, too. "Only the wisest people in the land will see this fabric," they said. "It will be invisible to fools and to those who are unfit for their office."

When the thieves opened their bags, the emperor squinted. He saw nothing at all in their hands! "Why, I must be a fool," thought the emperor. "Either that or I do not deserve to sit on this throne!" The emperor was embarrassed that he could not see the fabric, so he said, "That is the most magnificent fabric I have ever seen."

The emperor asked his wife what she thought of the magical fabric. She couldn't see anything, but she did not want anyone to think she was a fool, so she said, "It is quite extraordinary. It's like no other fabric that I know."

Knowing his wife was no fool, the emperor thought the fabric must be real, even though he could not see it. He offered the thieves twenty pieces of gold to make a new suit for him. They thanked the emperor and went to work right away.

"When you wear this suit, it will feel as light as a spider's web against your skin," one thief said as he measured the top of the emperor's head.

The other thief then explained, "You might even feel as though you're wearing nothing at all."

"I can't wait to try on my new suit," said the emperor excitedly. "It really sounds like it's the most wonderful fabric in the world!"

The thieves smiled slyly and winked at each other behind the emperor's back. They had finished sizing him up.

After a few days, the royal minister went to see how the new suit was coming along. He was going to tell the tailors to work as quickly as possible because the emperor was getting anxious. The minister was stunned by what he didn't see. The tailors were cutting away at the air with their scissors, and they were stitching up fabric that wasn't there! "Is it possible that I am a fool?" the minister gulped.

Seeing the minister, one of the thieves said, "Please tell the emperor that his suit will be ready soon. But first, please order another tray of food for us. All this hard work is making us very hungry."

That much must be true, the minister thought as he saw apple cores, chicken legs, and bits of cheese all over the floor. The thieves had eaten so much already, they must be working hard on something!

Finally the thieves brought the emperor his new suit. He put it on slowly, being careful not to snag the fine stitching he couldn't see. Then he strutted around the room. He had never felt so dashing.

"This is truly the finest suit I have ever had," the emperor said to the royal minister. "Tell me, what do you think of it?"

"If you are happy, then I am happy," said the royal minister, who was truly anything but happy. In his eyes, the emperor was standing in front of a mirror in his underwear, admiring a new suit that wasn't even there!

The emperor wanted to show off his new suit to everyone in the land. He asked the royal minister to call for a royal parade the next day.

"If that is what you want," said the minister, "then you shall have your parade."

Everyone in the kingdom was excited about the parade. They had long ago grown bored with all the stories of the emperor's clothes, but what interested them now was the new, magical fabric. They had all heard that fools could not see the fabric, and they wanted to find out who among them was a fool and who was not.

On the day of the parade, everyone pushed and shoved to get the best view. But when the emperor appeared, everyone was shocked. The emperor was in his underwear!

Nobody in the crowd could see the emperor's suit, but of course no one would admit it out loud. Nobody wanted to look like a fool. Instead the people said, "How handsome you look, your majesty. That certainly is a splendid suit. I never knew any fabric could look so wonderful."

Suddenly a young boy cried out over the noisy crowd. "The emperor isn't wearing a new suit!" he said. "What is everybody talking about? The emperor is wearing nothing but his underwear!"

The emperor quickly turned to look at the crowd. They stood in stunned silence. Instantly the emperor knew the boy was telling the truth. He realized that he had been a fool, and now he was parading himself throughout the kingdom in his underwear. Needless to say, the emperor felt quite embarrassed and quite foolish.

All at once everyone in the crowd began to laugh. They realized that they had all been foolish, too. They pretended to see a suit that was not even there because they were afraid of what the others would think. They felt silly for not telling the truth to the emperor.

After the parade, the embarrassed emperor quickly returned to the palace to put on some clothes. He ignored all of his fancy and frilly clothes and chose to put on a simple blue robe with plain yellow buttons. "Ah, that's better," the emperor said as he slipped on the robe. "I was beginning to get a chill from my new, magical suit." For the first time, the emperor left his room without looking in the mirror. Then he invited the honest young boy to speak with him in his court.

"I have decided to make you a junior minister. You have shown that you are very brave. You risked being called a fool to tell me the truth," the emperor said. "You will always be one of my most trusted friends."

"Thank you" the boy said. "I will always be honest with you, even if you don't like what I have to say."

"I'm counting on it," said the emperor.

One to Grow On

Honesty

Sometimes being honest means telling people things they don't want to hear. It's not always easy, and sometimes it's even scary to be honest. No matter how difficult it is, though, telling the truth is very important. It lets people know where they stand, and it helps keep them from making mistakes. If someone had been honest with the emperor earlier, he never would have made such a fool of himself.

Thank goodness for the honest little boy. If he had not told the truth, the emperor might still be ruling the kingdom in his underwear!

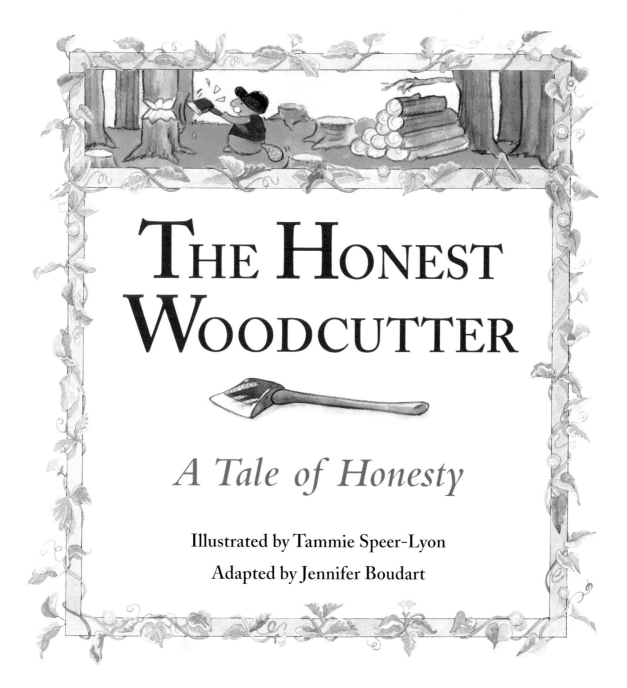

THE HONEST WOODCUTTER

A Tale of Honesty

Illustrated by Tammie Speer-Lyon

Adapted by Jennifer Boudart

There once was a woodcutter who lived with his wife and two children in a forest far from town. The woodcutter built his home with logs that he cut himself. The house was not big or fancy, but it was warm and dry. The family was not rich, but they were happy and lived comfortably.

One morning while eating breakfast, the family joked about what their lives would be like if they had lots of money. The woodcutter wished for a bigger house, his wife dreamed of eating from fine china plates, and the children imagined playing with all sorts of wonderful toys.

When breakfast ended, the woodcutter put on his hat, grabbed his ax, and headed to work. His family stood on the porch of the house and waved good-bye to him as he walked deep into the forest.

The woodcutter worked in the oldest part of the forest, where the trees grew tallest and thickest. These trees were also the hardest to chop down, but they were no problem for the woodcutter. He was the best around. The woodcutter simply sharpened his trusty old ax and went to work.

Soon wood chips flew through the air, and the forest echoed with the loud sound of the woodcutter's ax chopping. A little squirrel happened to be nearby collecting nuts, and she heard the noise of the woodcutter's ax. The squirrel went to see who was making all the noise and was amazed by how quickly the woodcutter chopped. She sat on a large pile of neatly stacked logs that the woodcutter had chopped earlier that morning. The woodcutter did not notice that the squirrel was sitting there. He thought only about cutting more wood so he could give his family all the things they wanted.

Each day the woodcutter worked until noon and then took a short break. He liked to walk to the edge of the river to catch his breath, eat lunch, and have a nice refreshing drink of water. The woodcutter never took too much time for lunch. He always wanted to get back to work. The more he worked, the more wood he could cut. And the more wood he cut, the better off his family would be.

This day, just like every other day, the woodcutter was taking his lunchtime break. He was very thirsty and walked quickly to the river to get a drink. If he had been paying more attention to where he was going, the woodcutter would have noticed a rock that was right in his path.

"Yikes!" shouted the woodcutter as he tripped over the rock. When he fell, the woodcutter's ax slipped out of his hands and landed in the middle of the river.

The woodcutter picked himself up and ran to the edge of the water. He looked into the river, hoping to see his ax, but it was no use! The river was fast and deep. The ax was probably long gone by now. Without his ax, the woodcutter could not chop wood. And without wood, he could not buy the things his family wanted. Without his ax, the woodcutter wouldn't even be able to buy food. The woodcutter hung his head and began to moan, "What am I going to do? That was my only ax! How can I earn a living for my family now?"

Suddenly the river started to make noise. The woodcutter looked up and saw the water rising. Then the water grew arms and a head, and it started to talk to him! "I am the water sprite, a fairy of this river. Why are you so sad?"

After the woodcutter told him what had happened, the water sprite said, "Don't worry. I can help you."

"I'll go down to the bottom of the river to find your ax," said the water sprite. In an instant the sprite was gone, and the river began to swirl and foam. After a few moments, the water sprite appeared again. This time the sprite smiled and held something in his watery hands. "Is this your ax?" he asked the woodcutter. "I found it in the rocks."

The woodcutter looked closely at the ax. Whoever owned it was rich indeed. The ax was so shiny and beautiful. It was made of pure silver! The woodcutter thought about taking it. He could sell the ax and buy many fine things for his family. There was just one problem, though. The ax did not belong to him, and it would be wrong to say it was his. Finally the woodcutter said, "I cannot take this ax. It is not mine."

The water sprite was surprised. He tossed the silver ax on the ground and said, "Very well, I'll look for your ax again."

Once again the sprite left to look for the woodcutter's ax at the bottom of the river. And once again the river began to swirl and foam. When the water sprite returned after a few moments, he held an ax that was more magnificent than the first one. It was made of solid gold! "This must be yours," said the sprite.

The woodcutter held the amazing gold ax for a moment. This ax could make him very rich. He could buy a big house in town, fine china dishes for his wife, and all the toys that his children could dream of! But the woodcutter gave the ax back to the sprite. "This is a fine ax, and you are kind to offer it to me," he explained. "But this ax is not mine. I am sure someone is looking for it and misses it."

The water sprite smiled and said, "Well, I see that you will take only your own ax. Let me look for it once more."

For a third time the magic water sprite left to look for the woodcutter's ax. When the sprite returned, he held another ax. This one was much different than the first two that he had brought to the woodcutter. This ax wasn't shiny at all, and the handle was worn from use. The woodcutter smiled and said, "Ah yes! This is my ax."

The water sprite shook his head. "Are you sure you want this ax? The other two are so much finer!"

"Yes, but they are not mine," said the woodcutter. He held his steel ax and said, "This ax has cut more trees than I can count. It was good enough for me before, so it must be good enough for me now."

The water sprite smiled and said, "Your ax is not worth much, but your honesty is. The silver and gold axes belong to me. I want you to take them as a gift for telling the truth."

The woodcutter was very excited to have all three axes. He thanked the water sprite and decided that he would leave the forest early that day. Instead of going straight home, he went into town to go shopping.

The woodcutter couldn't wait to get to the store. He was sure that the store owner would buy the gold and silver axes from him. When the woodcutter arrived, he handed the fine axes to the store owner. The owner looked them over carefully and finally said, "These are the best axes that I have ever seen. I will gladly buy them from you."

The store owner was very generous. He gave the woodcutter a large sack of gold coins. Now the woodcutter was rich! He bought an armful of beautiful flowers and a set of fine china plates for his wife. He also bought a big bag of toys for his children.

The woodcutter had lots of gold left over, and he carried it all back home with him. His wife and children were surprised that the woodcutter was home so early. They ran from the house to meet him. When the woodcutter's wife saw the china plates and the flowers, she was so happy that tears came to her eyes. When the children saw the big bag filled with toys, they squealed with joy.

The woodcutter told his family all that had happened to him during the day. That night, as he and his wife were putting the children to bed, his son looked up at him and asked, "Why did the water sprite give you all three axes?"

Then the woodcutter's daughter said, "Because you told the truth, right?"

"That's right," said the honest woodcutter, "because I told the truth."

One to Grow On

Honesty

Honesty means telling the truth, and it is always best to tell the truth. Sometimes, though, telling the truth is not so easy to do. When the water sprite handed the woodcutter the silver and gold axes, it would have been easy for the woodcutter to say that they belonged to him. But because he told the truth, the water fairy gave the woodcutter both of the valuable axes as a reward.

The story of the honest woodcutter reminds us that when you tell the truth, things always work out for the best. It shows that honesty really is the best policy.

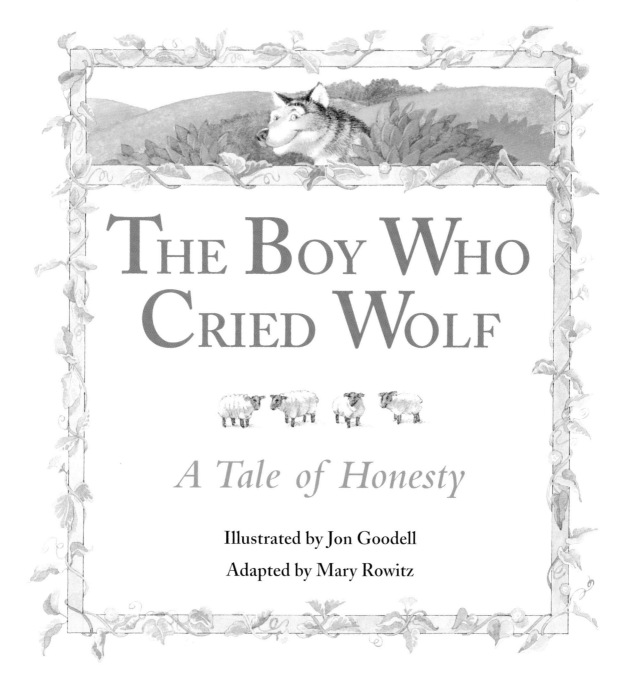

THE BOY WHO CRIED WOLF

A Tale of Honesty

Illustrated by Jon Goodell

Adapted by Mary Rowitz

There was a young boy who lived in a village. He wasn't very old, but he had an important job. He was a shepherd, and his job was to guard the sheep from danger, especially wolves.

The shepherd boy also had to make sure the sheep got plenty of food and exercise. Every day, in order to give the sheep the exercise they needed, the boy took them to a nearby valley. Once they had walked there, the sheep would graze on the tasty green grass that grew in the valley. The villagers trusted the shepherd to take good care of the sheep.

The shepherd boy wasn't really all alone. The village people worked nearby. If a wolf ever did attack, the people could run to the rescue.

The villagers counted on the shepherd boy to do his job. They never felt like they had to check on him. They trusted him to do what he was supposed to do.

Every day, the shepherd faithfully watched the sheep from his lookout post. He could also see the people hard at work. Some days they worked at their jobs in the village. Sometimes they did other chores.

For the shepherd boy, every day was the same. He looked at the sheep. They looked the same every day. Then he looked out at the forest. It looked the same, too. While he was happy most days just to do his job, some days he wished that something exciting would happen.

In his whole life, the boy had never seen a wolf come near the sheep. In fact, he had never even seen a wolf! Some people told stories of hearing wolves howl in the forest, but the boy never heard any howling. Sometimes he even wondered if there really were any wolves.

One day the shepherd tried to make things more exciting. He thought, "Maybe I can play some games with the sheep." He planned his next day, and he smiled when he thought about the fun he would have.

The boy woke up bright and early the next morning. He ate his breakfast very quickly and then packed his bag for the day. He kissed his parents good-bye and hurried to take the sheep to the valley.

As soon as they reached the green grass in the valley, the shepherd boy tried to play games with the sheep. The sheep, however, had a different idea. They didn't want to play catch. They weren't interested in trying to bounce the ball. They didn't even want to try to kick the ball.

All the sheep wanted to do was eat the grass or take a nap. "This isn't any fun at all," thought the shepherd boy.

Downhearted, the shepherd boy walked slowly back to his lookout post. "Alas," thought the boy, "I just wanted to make things a little more exciting around here."

Then something caught the corner of his eye. He could tell the wind was blowing because it made the treetops move. "I wonder," he said, thinking out loud, "what is on the other side of those trees?"

The boy smiled to himself. Would it be so bad to pretend there was a wolf? He thought this would be a good joke.

As the sheep ate the grass, he cupped his hand near his mouth and shouted, "Wolf! Wolf! A wolf is stealing the sheep! Come help me!"

All the village people stopped what they were doing and ran to help scare off the wolf. When they got there, they were very confused.

The villagers did not find a wolf. And where was the shepherd? They were worried about him. What if the wolf had stolen the boy? They frantically began to search high and low to find him.

A villager pointed to a tree and said, "There he is over there. Is he okay?" They saw he was not hurt. In fact, he was laughing!

"You looked so funny running up here for no reason. This was a great joke," laughed the boy.

The villagers did not laugh. They had been very scared for the boy and the sheep. They did not feel like laughing at all. They shook their heads and said, "We have to get back to work now. We don't have time for pranks."

The shepherd boy hardly heard a word they said. He was laughing too hard.

At breakfast the next day, the boy's mother and father told him to be good. He nodded his head and left to tend the sheep. Soon, however, he was bored again. "Wolf! Wolf!" he shouted, louder than the day before. "A wolf is stealing the sheep! Come help me!"

Again the villagers came running. Again there was no wolf in sight. This time the village people were very upset. They told the boy, "If you don't tell people the truth all the time, they will never know when to believe you."

The boy was still laughing at his joke. After the villagers went back to their jobs, however, he started to think about what the people had said. "Maybe," he thought, "it isn't so funny to play tricks on others." The shepherd boy began walking back to his lookout post. Little did he know he was soon going to have all the excitement he could handle.

Just on the other side of the trees, a sly wolf had seen everything. When the shepherd reached his post, the wolf began stealing the sheep. The shepherd couldn't believe his eyes. It was a real wolf! He cried out, "Wolf! Wolf! A wolf is stealing the sheep! Come help me!"

He waited for the villagers to come running, but no one came. They weren't going to fall for that trick again! This time, though, it was no trick.

The boy tried yelling for help again, but no one came. He could only watch as the wolf ran off into the forest with all the sheep. This time the only one laughing was the wolf.

The shepherd boy ran into the village. "Wolf! Wolf!" he cried. "He's stealing our sheep!" The boy kept running and calling for help, but no one believed he was telling the truth. He called out again, "Wolf! Wolf!"

"I bet!" said one villager. "I can't believe that boy is trying to make fools out of us again."

"Well, he's not going to make a fool out of me," said another villager. "I don't believe him."

Finally the shepherd boy stopped running. "I'm telling the truth this time," he said. "There really is a wolf in the valley, and he really is stealing the sheep. You've got to believe me."

The villagers came and looked at the boy. They shook their fingers at him. "We're smarter than you think," the people said. "This time we're just going to ignore you and your wolf! Humph!"

At that moment, the shepherd boy knew no one would believe him. How could he blame them? When they trusted him, he let them down. He lost their trust by not always telling the truth.

He sadly walked back to his lookout and gazed down where he always took his sheep to eat grass. But there weren't any sheep left. The wolf had taken all of them away. The boy was so sad that he began to cry.

The boy remembered what his parents and the villagers had told him. How he wished he had listened to what they said. He wished he had just always told the truth.

He didn't want any harm to come to the sheep! Because he didn't tell the truth, no one believed him when it really mattered. Now it was too late. The shepherd boy didn't think his joke was so funny anymore.

One to Grow On

Honesty

The shepherd boy learned the hard way about the importance of being honest. When he played tricks on the villagers, he paid a big price for a small joke. As much fun as it is to laugh, it is always important to tell the truth.

If you were one of the villagers, would you know when to believe the shepherd boy? How do you think it felt to be tricked? What are ways you can be sure people know you are telling the truth?

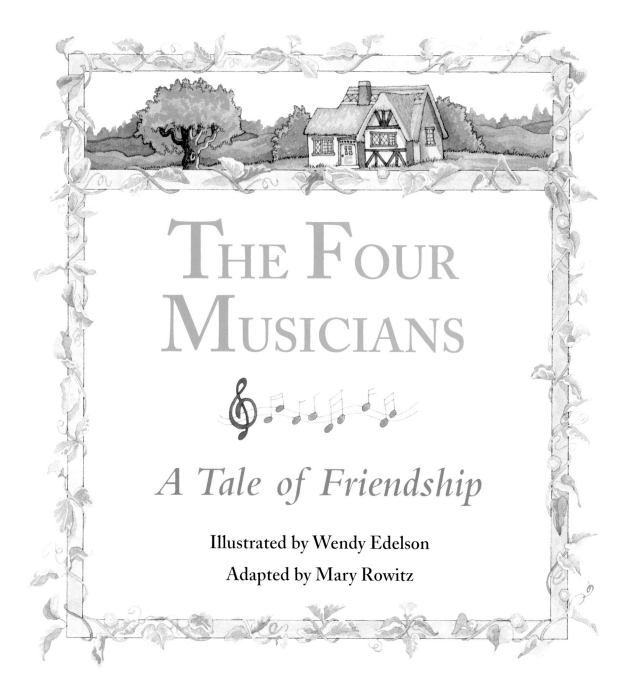

THE FOUR MUSICIANS

A Tale of Friendship

Illustrated by Wendy Edelson

Adapted by Mary Rowitz

One day a donkey was walking along the fence by the barn, singing softly to himself. He stopped when he heard his owner talking with another farmer. The donkey leaned in closer so he could better hear what the two were discussing. "I know what you mean," the one farmer said. "Sometimes it's easier to just get a younger one."

The donkey wondered what they could be talking about. His owner continued, "I just can't find many reasons to keep the tired bag of bones around much longer. He is very old and cannot pull the plow anymore. It's time to put that old donkey out to pasture."

The donkey couldn't believe his ears! They were talking about him! He was very hurt to hear these words. "Hee-haw!" said the donkey. "I won't be sent out to pasture. I'll go to the town of Bremen and become a musician."

The donkey had just started on his way when he saw a sad dog sitting by the road. The donkey asked what was bothering the dog. "My owner says I am too old to hunt," howled the dog. "He wants to get a younger dog who keeps quiet."

"I have a thought that may interest you. Why don't you come with me to Bremen, and we will work as musicians," said the donkey. "We'll be quite a team."

"Woof!" said the dog. "I really like that idea!" The two new pals had not gone far before they crossed paths with a gloomy cat. They asked what was wrong.

"My owner says I am too old to catch mice," he cried. "She is going to get a younger cat."

They invited the cat to come to Bremen to sing with them. "Mee-ow!" answered the cat, and the three were on their way.

The dog, cat, and donkey were walking along when suddenly a very upset rooster flew right into the middle of the road. "Cock-a-doodle-day!" the rooster squawked.

"What a strong voice you have!" the dog said.

"My owners say there is no point in having a strong voice if you don't use it every day," crowed the rooster. "I cannot get up early enough to wake up the workers anymore. My owners plan to serve me for Sunday dinner!"

"Join us on our trip," said the dog. "We are going to work as musicians. We could really use your strong voice to make our band complete."

"Cock-a-doodle-day!" said the rooster. "Let's be on our way!" The four new friends practiced singing as they walked toward Bremen.

Nighttime came. The donkey, dog, cat, and rooster had been singing and walking all day. Just when the four musicians found a nice tree to camp under, the rooster began to squawk. "I think I see a light shining from inside a house!" he said. "It doesn't seem far away."

"They might have some food to share," said the dog. "A big, juicy bone sounds mighty good right about now."

"Mmmm. I think a big bowl of milk would be absolutely purr-fect," purred the cat.

"A plate of corn certainly would hit the spot," crowed the rooster. The donkey thought it all sounded good, so the four set out for the house.

The four musicians walked up to the house. The donkey, being the tallest of the group, peered inside the window. After the donkey had looked through the glass for a few moments, the cat's curiosity got the better of him. "What do you see?" he asked as he tried to get a glimpse.

"Well, there are four men sitting at a table that is covered with food," the donkey said. "They must eat like kings every night. There are stacks of gold everywhere."

"What do we do now?" asked the rooster. "Do we just knock on the door and ask for food?"

The donkey shook his head. "Remember we are going to be musicians," he said. "We should practice singing for our supper." The others thought this was a grand idea, so they very carefully planned their first concert.

The four musicians decided to stand one on top of the other so everyone could be heard. First the donkey took his place near the bottom of the window. Then the dog jumped on his back. The cat made his way up to the dog's back. Finally the rooster flew to the top.

Even though the four friends had practiced their singing all day, they were still a little bit nervous. This was their first concert, after all. They wished each other good luck, turned to face the window, and cleared their throats. Finally their big moment had arrived. It was time to perform. The donkey gave the signal, and they began to sing.

Never has there been a louder or mightier group effort! The four friends tried to sing better than they ever had before. What they didn't know is that it didn't sound like singing. It sounded like, "Hee-haw! Woof! Mee-ow! Cock-a-doodle-day!"

The four friends also did not know that the men inside were robbers. They were hiding out and counting gold they had stolen. When they heard the loud noise, they looked out the window. They saw what looked like a four-headed beast. "Run! Run! Run!" one robber yelled. "Run before the four-headed beast gets us!"

The animals were confused. Why had the men run away? The donkey said, "I believe I know what is happening. No doubt our audience enjoyed our singing so much that they must be going to get more people to hear our concert."

"It may be some time before they return. I say we go inside and have some dinner as a reward for our splendid singing," the rooster said.

"Indeed!" agreed the donkey. "That is a grand idea!" The four musicians went into the house.

The four musicians were so hungry that they ate every last bite! It didn't take long to decide that the life of a musician was going to suit them very well indeed. Soon after the meal, they were very sleepy. Since they were already inside the house, they agreed it would be best to spend the night there. After all, they didn't want to miss the people who were going to come hear them perform.

There was plenty of room for everyone in the house. The donkey lay in the middle of the room. The dog stretched out by the door. The cat curled up near the fireplace, and the rooster flew to a ceiling beam.

Soon their sleepy heads began nodding. It didn't take long for their tired eyes to close. They were all sound asleep when the door knob slowly began to turn. They were still asleep when someone tiptoed into the room.

One robber had come back to see if he could get at least some of the gold. It was quite dark, and he needed some light in order to find his way around. He thought he saw a glow from the coals in the fireplace. But the glow wasn't from the coals. It was the cat's eyes. When he lit a match to start a fire, the cat jumped up. The robber tripped over the dog. The dog bit his leg, causing the robber to stumble over the donkey. The donkey kicked the robber. The noise woke the rooster, and he began crowing, "Cock-a-doodle-day! Leave without delay!"

The robber ran as fast as his legs would carry him. He told the others to stay away forever or the four-headed beast would get them.

The four musicians lived in the house for the rest of their days. They were quite happy giving free concerts and using the gold to buy food.

Friendship

The four musicians learned a great deal about friendship. At first they each felt sad and alone. Once they made friends with each other, they were much happier. When the four musicians started thinking about all the good things they could do together, they stopped feeling so sad.

How do you feel when a friend helps you? How do you feel when you help a friend? Is there someone you know who could use a friend?

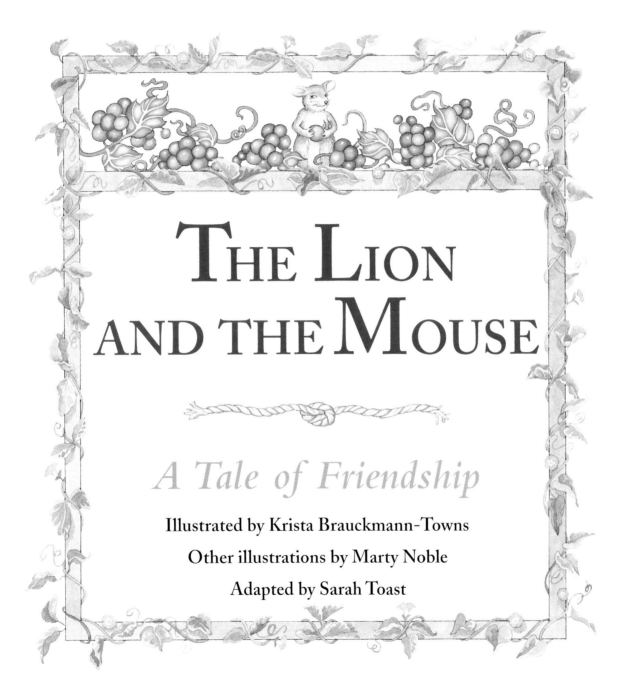

THE LION AND THE MOUSE

A Tale of Friendship

Illustrated by Krista Brauckmann-Towns

Other illustrations by Marty Noble

Adapted by Sarah Toast

One day a lion was taking a nice nap in the warm sun. Nearby, a busy little mouse scurried about looking for berries, but all the berries were too high for her to reach. Then the mouse spotted a lovely bunch of berries that she could reach by climbing the rock below them. When she did, the mouse discovered that she hadn't climbed a rock at all. She had climbed right on top of the lion's head!

The lion did not like to be bothered while he was sleeping. He awoke with a loud grumble. "Who dares to tickle my head while I'm taking a nap?" roared the lion.

The mouse could see how angry the lion was with her, so she jumped off his head and started to run away. The lion grabbed for the little mouse as quickly as he could, but she was too quick and he just missed her.

The quick little mouse hurried to get away from the lion. She zigged and zagged through the grass, but the lion was always just one step behind. At last the lion chased the mouse right back to where they had started. The poor little mouse was too tired to run anymore, and the lion scooped her up in his huge paw.

"Little mouse," roared the lion. "Don't you know that I am the king of the forest? Why did you wake me up from my pleasant nap by tickling my head?"

"Oh please, lion," said the mouse. "I was only trying to get some lovely berries."

"Just see how much you like it when I tickle your head," said the lion.

"Please, lion," pleaded the mouse. "If you spare me, I am sure I will be able to help you some day."

Suddenly the lion began to smile, and then he began to laugh. "How could you, a tiny mouse, help the most powerful animal in the forest?" he chuckled. "That's so funny, I'll let you go—this time."

Then the lion laughed some more. He rolled over on his back, kicking and roaring with laughter. The mouse had to leap out of his way to avoid being crushed. Off she ran.

Still chuckling, the lion got up and realized he was hungry. He set out to find some lunch, and it wasn't long before he smelled food. Walking toward the good smell, the lion got caught in a trap set by hunters.

The lion was stuck in the strong ropes, and the more he struggled, the tighter they held him. Fearing the hunters would soon return, the terrified lion roared for help.

The mouse heard the lion's roars from far away. At first she was a little afraid to go back, thinking the lion might hurt her. But the lion's cries for help made the mouse sad, and she remembered the promise she made to help him. The mouse hurried to where the lion was tangled in the trap.

"Oh lion," said the mouse. "I know what it feels like to be caught. But you don't need to worry. I'll try to help you."

"I don't think there's anything you can do," said the lion. "These ropes are very strong. I've pushed and pulled with all my might, but I can't get free."

Suddenly the mouse said, "I have an idea! Just hold still, and I'll get to work." She quickly began chewing through the thick ropes with her small, sharp teeth. She worked and worked, and before long, the mouse had chewed through enough rope for the lion to get out of the trap!

Soon the lion wriggled out of the trap. He was very grateful to the mouse. "Mouse," he said, "I thank you for saving me, and I am sorry that I laughed at you before."

Then the lion scooped up the mouse and placed her on his head. He carried her back to the berry bush and lay down under it. "Mouse," he said, "I want you to reach up and pick one of those berries that you wanted earlier today."

The mouse plucked the biggest berry she could find. The lion took the mouse off of his head and held her in his paw. "Let's stick together," he said. "I can help you reach the berries, and you can get me out of a tight spot now and then."

"Okay!" said the mouse, and they've been friends ever since.

One to Grow On

Friendship

Friendship is a wonderful virtue. The more people you share it with, the better it is. Everyone likes to spend time with old friends. In this story, the lion and the mouse discover how much fun it is to make new friends.

Sometimes, though, it's hard to be friends. At first the lion was angry with the mouse and did not want to be friends. The mouse was afraid because the lion was mean and had laughed at her. In the end the lion and the mouse learn that it's better to be nice than to be mean. They find out that even though they are very different, they can still be good friends.

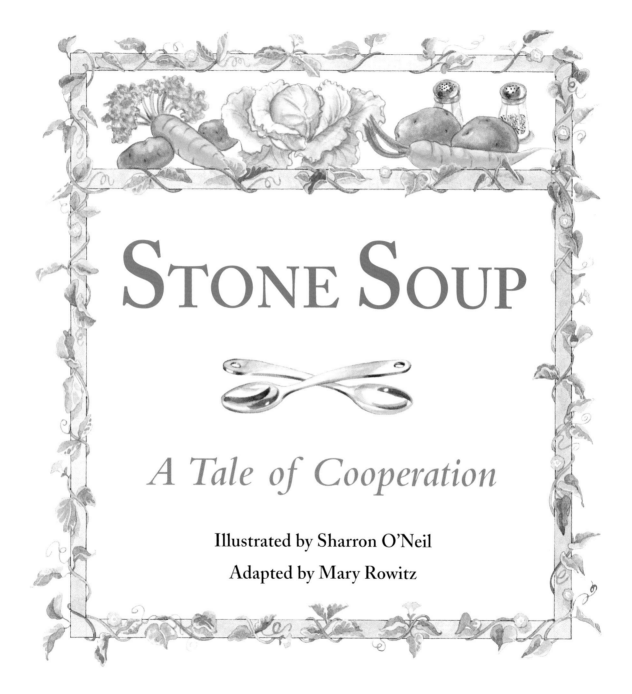

STONE SOUP

A Tale of Cooperation

Illustrated by Sharron O'Neil

Adapted by Mary Rowitz

A hungry traveler had been roaming the countryside for a long time, and he hadn't eaten a good meal in quite a while. One day the traveler spotted a lovely village off in the distance. The hungry traveler became very excited and said to himself, "I'm bound to find someone in the village who will share a meal with me."

As the traveler hurried to the town, he tripped over a stone in the road. The stone was not like any that the traveler had ever seen before. It was perfectly smooth and oval in shape. The traveler looked at the stone carefully and decided he would keep it. "You never know when a stone like this might come in handy," he said.

Then the traveler happily headed to the village. His empty stomach grumbled as he walked.

When the traveler arrived in the village, things did not go as well as he had hoped. He stopped at a few houses with no luck finding a meal. No one had any food to share. One house the traveler came to was very quiet. All the doors and windows were closed, and the shades were drawn. The traveler began to think that no one was home. Finally a maid appeared in the doorway. "Can you spare some food?" the traveler asked her. "I have been traveling for days and am very hungry."

"I'm sorry, but I have only a few potatoes," the maid said. "There's not enough to spare or share. Why don't you try my neighbor next door?"

"I already have," said the traveler, "but he was very grumpy and just slammed the door. It looks like finding some food in this village will be more difficult than I thought." Still the hungry traveler refused to give up.

The traveler visited every house in the village, but no one had enough food to spare or share. At one house there was only cabbage, the next had only carrots, and a third had only salt and pepper.

Since there was no food for the hungry traveler, he decided to move on. Before he got very far, the traveler began to feel tired. He decided to get some rest in the cool shade of a tree just outside the village. As he sat under the tree, the traveler looked back at the quiet little town. "It's a shame," he thought, "such a nice village and such a beautiful day, but nobody is outdoors talking or playing."

Then the traveler reached into his bag and took out the smooth, oval stone that he found earlier in the day. As he sat admiring the stone, the traveler suddenly had a brilliant idea!

The traveler ran back to the village and shouted, "Come out of your houses, everybody! I have a magic stone, and it will give us enough food for a wonderful meal. Everyone in town will have plenty to eat, and there will even be enough to spare and share!" One by one, the curious villagers peeked out of their doors and windows.

The grumpy villager who slammed the door on the traveler earlier looked out of his window and shouted, "What's all the racket about?"

"Come help me make a pot of delicious stone soup," said the traveler.

The maid stepped out of her house as two excited children ran up to the traveler. "Is that your stomach I hear growling?" one child asked.

"Yes," the other replied, "I am very hungry."

"Does anybody have a large soup kettle to get us started?" the traveler asked.

"I've got one that you can use," said the big, grumpy villager, "but I don't think it will do any good. I don't think your magic stone will really work."

Most of the villagers were excited, but some felt the same way as the big, grumpy villager. "Do you really believe he can make soup from a stone?" asked one young lady.

"I guess we'll find out soon," said another. "I certainly hope he can. I haven't had good soup in a long time."

The grumpy villager brought out his large kettle and placed it on a pile of sticks for the fire. "Here you go," he said. "Now let's see if that magic stone of yours can really make enough soup for all of us."

"Don't worry," said the traveler. "There will be plenty."

The traveler placed the smooth, oval stone into the kettle of water and began to stir. After a little while he tasted the soup. "Not bad," the traveler said, "but I think it could use a little salt and pepper."

"I've got some," said one of the young ladies. "I'll run home and get it."

"Perhaps the soup would taste even better if I shared my potatoes," the maid suggested.

"Yes, that's a great idea," said the traveler. "Why don't you get them, and we'll add them right away."

The young lady returned and sprinkled her salt and pepper into the kettle. Then the maid came back and dropped in her potatoes. Once again the traveler stirred the stone soup. When he tasted it for the second time, all the villagers watched him with anticipation.

"This is very good, but it would taste even better with some carrots and cabbage," said the traveler. Then a young boy ran home to get some carrots, and a little girl ran home to get her cabbage.

By now, everyone was having so much fun that they forgot how hungry they were. Even the big, grumpy villager was no longer grumpy. "Let's make this meal a party!" he shouted.

The girl returned with the cabbage, and the boy soon followed with his carrots. "Just think, a huge kettle of soup made from a magic stone," said the boy. "I can't wait to try it!"

"Neither can I," said the girl.

Finally the traveler announced that the
stone soup was ready to eat. He filled all the bowls,
and the villagers began to eat. Afterward there was plenty
of soup left over. "There's enough to spare and share!" said
the young lady.

The villagers were so happy after dinner that they
didn't want the evening to end. They started playing music
together and dancing with one another. At last the village
was alive with chatter and laughter.

"I didn't know you could play the banjo," the maid said to
the big villager.

"And I didn't know you could play the washboard," he
responded.

"I think there was a lot we didn't know until the traveler
came along," said the maid.

The next morning, the traveler said good-bye to his new friends in the village. It was time for him to leave. "I want you to have this," the traveler said as he handed the smooth, oval stone to the villagers. "Now you will always be able to make stone soup together, and you will never be hungry or sad or grumpy again." Each of the villagers hugged the traveler and told him to come back and visit some time. They were all very grateful and hoped to see the traveler again.

As the traveler headed out of the lovely little village, he  stumbled over another stone in the road. He picked it up at once and admired its dark, jagged edges. The traveler looked at the stone carefully and finally decided to keep it. "You never know when a stone like this might come in handy," he said to himself as he placed it in his bag.

Cooperation

Cooperation means working with others to do things that need doing. In this story the hungry traveler used the smooth, oval stone to show the villagers how to cooperate. When the traveler came to town, each of the villagers had a little bit of food but not enough for an entire meal. The traveler helped the villagers work together to make a delicious soup. When they cooperated, the villagers found they had plenty of food for everyone.

Cooperation can make difficult things easy, and it can also be lots of fun. The villagers learned that it's easy to make friends when you cooperate.

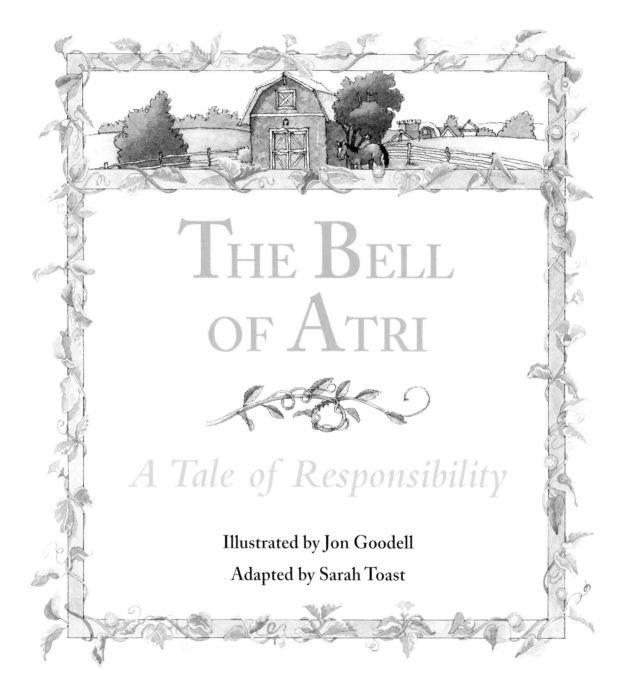

THE BELL OF ATRI

A Tale of Responsibility

Illustrated by Jon Goodell

Adapted by Sarah Toast

Long ago in a little town called Atri, smack dab in the center of town, there hung a bronze bell. The townspeople called it the bell of justice. It was no ordinary bell. It wasn't rung on holidays or the mayor's birthday. This bell was to be rung only when someone who had been treated unfairly needed help to right the wrong.

The people of Atri were proud of their bell. They kept it polished so bright that it looked like gold in the shining sun. Anyone—rich or poor, young or old, tall or short—could pull on the long rope and ring the bell to have their story heard. When the mayor heard the bell ring, he would put on his special robe and call for his assistant. All the people would gather in the town square to see how the mayor set things right again.

Most of the time, the people of Atri treated each other fairly and honorably, so the bell was hardly ever rung. After many years, however, time took its toll on the bell's rope. The rope had worn away so much that only the tallest person could ring it—certainly not a child.

One day the mayor was on his tour of the town. He liked to walk around and greet all the townspeople. On this day, the mayor saw the sorry state of the bell's rope. "This will never do," exclaimed the mayor. "We need a new rope immediately!" Everyone searched high and low, but they could not find a rope that was long enough. The mayor had to send for a new, long rope from the town on the other side of the mountain.

Meanwhile the mayor's assistant brought a long, tough grapevine from his fields. It would have to serve as a bell pull until the new rope arrived.

On a farm just outside of the city limits lived an old knight. His glory days on the field of battle were long since over. Now he spent his time out on the farm. The knight had once owned beautiful horses and hunting dogs, for he had taken great delight in hunting foxes and deer.

Now the old knight hardly ever hunted. He had sold his dogs and all his horses but one. That one horse served the knight faithfully in many battles in his youth, so the knight kept that horse for when he had to make a fine appearance at a festival or in a holiday parade.

Although the old knight had plenty of money, he no longer was willing to spend it to take proper care of his farm or his one, old horse. He preferred to spend his time sitting at his table and counting his money instead.

The knight didn't care that the stable was falling down and the poor horse didn't get any attention. The day finally came when the old knight wouldn't even buy his horse enough food to eat. The horse tried not to make too much of a fuss, but his tummy was empty.

The knight decided not to keep the horse any longer. He opened the pasture gate and sent the horse out to wander the countryside. It was a hot summer, and the sun had dried up the grass. The horse did not understand what was happening. He only knew he was hungry. When he couldn't find enough to eat at the side of the road, he didn't know what to do.

The hungry horse went from farm to farm looking for something to eat, but there were fences around the fields. The horse could not reach any of the hay or fresh grass. He just kept walking.

Not wanting to be a bother, the horse did his best to stay out of everyone's way. He wandered the back roads to find some grass to nibble, but he couldn't find enough. He became thinner and thinner.

One day the horse was trudging slowly along the road into the town of Atri. He was feeling very sad. The horse walked along with his head hanging low, hoping to spot a tuft of grass or two. A nibble here, a nibble there, and without knowing it, he was at the edge of the town.

He looked up from his place on the road. The horse could see right into the center of town. Then something caught the hungry horse's eye. He craned his neck forward to be sure he was seeing correctly. Sure enough, there was a juicy green vine hanging down from a bell. A bright green leaf almost touched the ground. The horse couldn't believe his eyes.

The bright leaf looked especially delicious to the hungry horse. He went the rest of the way into the square. No one was in sight, so he walked right up to the green vine. He took the lowest leaf in his mouth, closed his eyes, and began to chew.

The leaf was so tender, and it tasted so good! He couldn't remember the last time he had eaten anything so delicious. The hungry horse then worked his way up the vine to the next leaf and ate that. He began eating faster. When the horse had finished eating the leaves within reach, he began to pull on the vine so he could reach the leaves that were higher up.

When the old horse pulled on the vine, the bell of Atri rang out loud and clear. It seemed to say, "Ding dong! The knight did wrong!"

The good people of Atri heard the bell of justice ringing. They quickly gathered in the town square to find out who had been wronged. When the mayor heard the bell, he put on his robe, and called for his assistant. "We must go and make sure justice is served," said the mayor. They went to the bell.

The people were astonished at the sight of the old horse tugging at the vine. The horse was so hungry he didn't even notice the people. "I remember this horse," said the mayor. "This is the old knight's horse. This noble steed served the knight well for years in many a fierce battle. He was always a brave and loyal horse."

"Now he is a hungry horse without a good home," said a little girl.

"The horse deserves justice just as much as any person," said the mayor. "Send for the knight!"

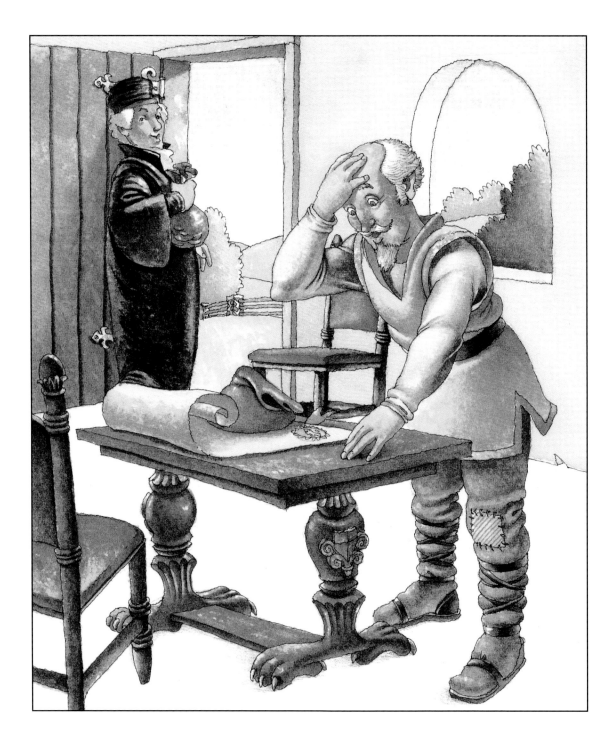

The knight was brought to the square. Then the mayor looked at him and began his address. "Knight," said the mayor, "this horse was your faithful servant for years when he was young. Now that he is old, you have turned him away to find food and shelter for himself, even though you have plenty of money to care for him."

The townsfolk shouted, "Hear, hear!"

The mayor continued, "Knight, I hereby decree that you should pay for this horse to be properly sheltered and fed for the rest of his life."

The townsfolk cheered, "Hip! Hip! Hooray!" They knew justice had been served.

At the knight's home, the mayor's assistant took enough of the knight's gold to pay for the proper care of the horse for the rest of his days.

The people of Atri used some of the knight's money to build a new stable for the horse. They took turns making sure the old horse always had plenty of hay and fresh water.

The children were especially fond of the old hero. They were always coming to feed him a tasty carrot or sugar cube. Sometimes they would ride on the horse's back and pretend that they were knights. The horse felt very loved, and he was very happy.

Just as before, the people of Atri were for the most part honest and decent. They treated each other well, so the bell of Atri was seldom rung. But the story of how the old horse rang the bell for justice was told often.

One to Grow On

Responsibility

The horse had served the knight well for a long time, and now it was the knight's responsibility to take good care of the horse. A person whose life has been made better by the acts of another should help that other person when help is needed. We all have a responsibility to one another.

Returning care or helping someone brings a sense of joy and strength to the helper. Think of a time someone has helped you. Is there someone you can help? Keep your eyes open for the chance to pitch in and help someone out. It feels good to be responsible!

THE GIFT

A Tale of Generosity

Illustrated by Debbie Dieneman

Adapted by Jennifer Boudart

Percy and Amelia were twin bear cubs. That meant that the brother and sister shared the same birthday. They didn't mind sharing. They really liked it. The twins found that when they shared something, they had twice as much fun. They shared almost everything, even their playtime.

They loved playing outdoors. When the weather was nice, they would dash outside as soon as they got permission. Percy loved to fly the kite his father helped him make. He had even tied the kite's tail himself.

Amelia loved looking through her binoculars. They had been a gift from her Aunt Ruth. The binoculars hung around Amelia's neck wherever she went. When she was outside, she was always searching the trees through her trusty binoculars. Percy's eyes were always on his kite as it danced in the sky.

One day, Percy stood at the edge of the forest, holding the kite's string in his hands. He watched as the kite flew in the sky. He had been practicing some new tricks with the kite. When he pulled back on the string, the kite would jump through the air as if it were dancing. The kite's streaming tail twisted back and forth in the breeze.

Percy knew to keep his toy away from the trees. In the past he had climbed more than a few trees to rescue the kite from branches. The kite's tail was now torn and a bit muddy. Sometimes the knots came loose. In fact, if you looked closely, you could tell that the tail wasn't as long as it used to be. Once it had gotten stuck in a bush. When that happened, Percy had to cut off part of the tail. He did his very best to patch it up. It was the only kite tail he had. Only his care kept the old kite flying.

Amelia sometimes pretended that she was a nature explorer. She used her binoculars to spot the birds hiding among the leaves. One day she saw three beautiful birds in one tree. She pretended they were rare African eagles. For the entire afternoon, she followed them everywhere they went. After several hours, it seemed as though they had led her through most of the forest. Finally Amelia had to go home.

Because she looked through her binoculars so much, Amelia saw a lot of things that others probably missed. That was one reason they were so special to her. Every night before she went to bed, Amelia faithfully cleaned off her binoculars and polished the glass lenses very carefully. Then she slipped

the special binoculars underneath her pillow. It was the only safe place she could think of to keep them.

The day before their birthday, Amelia sat alone in the room she shared with Percy. Their birthday party was planned for the next day. When she had been at the store a few weeks ago, she had found the perfect gift. There was a brand new kite tail hanging on the wall of the store. It was the most beautiful kite tail Amelia had ever seen. It was much longer than Percy's homemade tail had ever been. She thought it would keep Percy's kite flying high for many years.

Amelia started saving her money the first day she saw the kite tail in the shop. Now she hoped she had enough in her savings to buy it. Amelia slowly emptied out her bank and counted the coins. She did not have enough money to buy the gift! Amelia stretched out on her bed and thought. Suddenly she had an idea!

Amelia quickly jumped off her bed and asked her mother for permission to go shopping. Then she raced to the shop as fast as she could. She went to the checkout counter. "Can I help you, young lady?" asked the shopkeeper.

"I sure hope so," answered Amelia, setting down the binoculars. "Would you buy these?"

The shopkeeper looked at the binoculars carefully. He could tell someone had taken good care of them. He slowly rubbed his beard and said, "I think we can make a deal." He handed Amelia a big pile of crisp dollar bills. Right away she used the money to buy Percy's gift. She even had enough left over to buy special wrapping paper. On her way home, Amelia held the gift close to her. As she walked, she thought about how the binoculars used to feel around her neck. She would miss them, but her brother was worth it.

Later that day Percy walked into the same shop. He had spent almost the entire morning flying his kite and thinking. A few weeks ago something very special had been delivered to the shop. The instant he saw it, he knew it was the perfect gift for his sister. It was a carrying case for binoculars. The case was lined with velvet and had a lock and key. "Now," he thought, "Amelia will finally have a safe place to store her binoculars." There was one problem, Percy didn't have any money for the gift. But now he did have a plan. He walked up to the shopkeeper. "I want to sell my kite," announced Percy.

The shopkeeper looked it over. "Well, I see it's in need of a new tail, but I think I can take care of that," he said. They made a deal, and Percy left with the gift tucked under his arm. He used to carry his kite that way. Percy would miss the kite, but his sister was worth it.

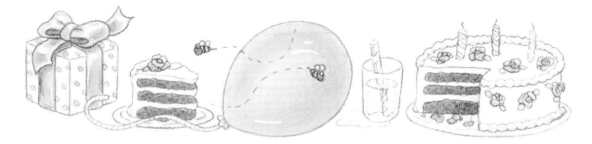

Finally it was the day of the party. Amelia was excited but nervous, too. She could not wait for Percy to open the gift she had found for him. But what if he found out she had sold her binoculars? Would he get upset? She would just have to tell him he was the best kite flyer in the world, and he should have the best kite tail ever. It made her happy do something nice for him.

When Amelia walked in the front door, Percy was waiting for her. Amelia smiled at her brother and shouted out, "Happy birthday, Percy!"

"Happy birthday, Amelia!" Percy shouted back.

Their parents lit the candles and everyone sang "Happy Birthday." The twins closed their eyes and made their wishes. Then they blew out the candles and ate a piece of cake. Finally it was time to open up the presents. Ripping open the wrapping paper, they were very surprised at what was inside. Percy didn't want Amelia to know about the kite, so he said, "Get your binoculars and try out the case!"

Amelia didn't want Percy to know about her binoculars. "Don't you love your new kite tail? I just had to buy it for you. Go get your kite!"

Percy sighed out loud. Then he said, "Amelia, I'm so sorry. I sold the kite to buy your gift."

Now Amelia's mouth dropped open. "I'm sorry, too. I sold my binoculars to buy your gift!"

The twins laughed and laughed at what had happened. When they could finally stop laughing, they said to each other, "I just wanted you to be happy!" Then they hugged one another and laughed again.

"I think trying to make someone happy is the best gift of all," said their mother. "Don't forget, you still have other gifts to open."

"I know," said Amelia. "Let's finish our party outside. We'll take our presents and cake to the forest for a picnic!"

The twins packed the picnic basket and went to find the perfect spot for their picnic. Later their family joined them, and everyone played games. After a fun-filled day, they went home. The twins gave everyone a kiss and hug. As they settled into their bear cub beds that night, Amelia and Percy agreed this was the best birthday they ever had.

One to Grow On

Generosity

Generosity is about giving to others without thinking of yourself. Amelia and Percy were very generous. Their love for each other made it easy to part with something that meant a lot to them.

In this story Percy and Amelia remind us that being generous to others is rewarding. Can you think of a time when someone was generous to you? Can you think of ways to show generosity?

THE SELFISH GIANT

A Tale of Generosity

Illustrated by Sherry Neidigh

Adapted by Mary Rowitz

Every day after school, a group of children who lived near a huge, empty castle played in its enchanted garden. The garden was enchanted because it stayed summer there all year long. The trees in the enchanted garden never lost their leaves, flowers bloomed all year, and it never got cold there. Sometimes it rained in the garden, but only at nighttime when the children were sleeping soundly in their beds.

The children skipped rope, swung from the tree branches, and played games in the enchanted garden. When they got hungry, they plucked fruit from the trees and ate it as they enjoyed the sunshine that never ended.

The children were happiest when they were in the garden. They loved to play there every day.

The empty castle did not stay empty for long. It belonged to a giant who had been away for many years. One day he returned home hoping to find some peace and quiet after his long journey.

Instead he returned to the sound of laughter in his garden. He did not like what he saw when he looked over the garden wall. There were children playing all sorts games and eating the fruit from his trees.

"What are you children doing here?" the giant shouted. "This is *my* garden!"

The giant's booming voice startled the children. They were so shaken that they could not answer his question. But then, the giant was in no mood to listen to reasons why he should share his garden.

He was a selfish giant.

The giant stormed into the garden and ordered all the children to leave at once. "Get down from those trees!" he roared. "Get out of my garden and never come back!"

The children didn't understand why the giant wanted them to leave. No one had ever sent them away. The children were frightened of the grumpy giant, and they ran from the garden as fast as they could.

Once the children were gone, the giant looked around the empty garden and smiled. Finally he would have some peace and quiet. "No noise, no pesky children running around," he muttered to himself. "Just me and my garden."

He was a very selfish giant.

The children no longer had a place to play. They tried playing in other yards and gardens, but no place compared to their enchanted garden.

One day they stopped outside the garden wall. They thought that if they could at least be close to the garden, they would once again be happy. One curious boy wanted to see the garden with his own eyes, so he climbed onto a friend's shoulders and peeked over the garden wall. The boy gasped at what he saw. The leaves of trees were turning orange and were falling to the ground. The grass that was once thick and green was now thin and brown. The flowers had wilted, and the birds had flown away.

"What has happened to our wonderful garden? It looks like it is dying," said one child. All the children became sad. Their beautiful garden was no longer enchanted.

Soon the garden became a cold and lonely place. All the trees were bare, the grass was the color of straw, and the sun never shone there anymore.

One day, as the giant passed in front of a castle window overlooking the garden, a flower poked its head through the ground. The giant watched the flower. He began to hope it would bloom.

But then a strong gust of wind came and scared the flower back under the ground. The giant sighed. He didn't understand the changes that had taken place in his garden. When he returned from his journey, the garden was warm and full of life, but now it was dull and cold.

"At least now I have peace and quiet," the giant said, "and I don't have to share the garden with anyone."

The giant was simply being selfish.

The passing months brought even more changes to the garden. Snow blanketed the ground, icicles dangled from the walls of the castle, and cold winds ripped through the branches of the trees.

The giant now spent many hours of his day watching the garden from the castle window. The giant could not figure out why it was so cold inside the walls of his garden. He knew that it was no longer wintertime, and the rest of the countryside was warm, not covered with snow.

"Something is not right," the giant said. He began to wish for his beautiful garden and for the children who had made it such a happy place. For the first time, the giant felt lonely.

By now the children had surely found another place to play, the giant thought. They no longer needed his garden to make them happy.

The giant was wrong. The children stopped outside the garden every day, wishing they could play there again.

One day, as a child leaned against the garden wall, a stone wiggled loose and fell out. The hole it left was big enough to crawl through. The children looked at each other excitedly and crawled through the secret passage one by one.

When their feet touched the ground, the snow in the garden began to melt. The grass turned green, and the sun began to shine again. When the children touched the trees, green leaves appeared. The birds came back and sang pretty songs. The children were filled with joy to be back in the enchanted garden.

But in a small corner of the garden, icicles still hung from a single tree. A little boy looked up at the tree sadly. He wanted to climb it, but he was too small to reach the lowest branch.

The little boy anxiously circled the tree. Then he stopped and looked up at the high branches. He had waited such a long time to play in the trees in the enchanted garden. Now that he had the chance, he could not reach even the lowest branch. The boy sat down under the tree and began to cry.

Suddenly the boy felt a huge pair of hands gently lift him up and set him on one of the branches. Instantly the icicles that clung to the tree began to melt. Then tiny buds opened, and leaves sprouted all over the tree.

The surprised little boy turned to see the giant who had once roared with anger at the children. This time the giant smiled and patted the little boy on the head.

The boy flung his arms around the giant's neck and kissed him on the cheek. The giant's heart melted as quickly as the ice and snow in his garden. He was sorry he had been so selfish.

When the other children saw that they no longer had to fear the giant, they rushed over to him. The giant scooped them up one by one and hugged them gently.

"Does this mean that we may sometimes play in your enchanted garden?" asked one shy child. The other children quietly waited to hear what the giant would say.

The giant now realized that it was the children who brought the magic to his garden. "From now on this is your garden," the giant said to the children. "You may come here to play whenever you wish."

The enchanted garden was more fun than ever. The giant was no longer selfish. In fact he became the chidren's favorite playmate. The children loved every minute they spent in the garden. And so did the giant—he had the most enchanted time of all.

One to Grow On

Generosity

The giant refused to share his garden with the children because he was selfish. He wanted peace and quiet, and when he sent the children away, he got plenty of that. But he also got something more: loneliness. The giant finally realized that the children were not a nuisance. They brought beauty to the garden and joy to his heart.

The giant came to know this joy only after he decided to share his garden with the children. In the end, he was a very generous and happy giant.

This story reminds us that sharing your belongings can be much more fun than keeping them to yourself.

THE UGLY DUCKLING

A Tale of Patience

Illustrated by Susan Spellman

Other illustrations by Marty Noble

Adapted by Sarah Toast

Once upon a time, on a lovely spring day in the country, something exciting was about to happen. A mother duck was sitting on her nest by the edge of the pond. She had been sitting there for a very long time waiting for her eggs to hatch. It seemed like she had been sitting there forever!

Finally the eggs began to crack. "Peep, peep," said the newly hatched ducklings. "Quack, quack," said their mother. "You are the sweetest little yellow ducklings that I have ever seen! Are you all here?" She stood up to look in the nest. She saw that the biggest egg hadn't hatched yet.

The tired mother duck sat down again on the last egg. When it finally cracked open, out tumbled a clumsy, gray baby bird. He was bigger than the others, and he didn't look like them. In fact, compared to other baby ducks, he was rather funny looking.

"Peep, peep," said the big baby. The mother duck looked at him. "He's awfully big for his age," she thought to herself. "I wonder if he can swim?"

The next day, the sun was shining brightly. The mother duck led her ducklings to the pond. "Quack, quack," she told them, and the ducklings understood. One after the other, the eager little ducklings jumped into the water. They bobbed and floated like little corks. They knew how to paddle their legs and swim without being told.

All of the new baby birds swam very nicely, even the one who looked different. "He may have too long a neck," thought the mother duck, "but see how nicely he holds it. If you tilt your head a little bit, he is almost handsome." For the rest of the afternoon, the mother duck helped the baby ducklings practice their swimming.

The mother duck was very happy with her ducklings. She decided it was time to take her babies to the farm to meet the other ducks. "Quack, quack," said the mother duck. "Follow me! Keep your legs far apart and waddle."

The one baby could not quite get it right. The other baby ducks on the farm gathered around him and said, "Look how ugly that duckling is!" One big duck came over and quacked, "Stay out of my way, you ugly duckling!"

"Leave him alone!" cried the mother duck. "He may not be good-looking, but he is kind and he can swim as well as anyone—maybe even better!" No one listened to her. The other ducks acted mean and chased the poor ugly duckling.

A few days later, the other ducklings were playing on the farm. They wouldn't let the ugly duckling join in any of the games. For a while, the little duckling sat all alone. Then he got an idea. "I'll practice my swimming!" he said to himself.

The ugly duckling went to the pond and swam and swam and swam. When he stopped, he was very tired. Then he looked around. The ugly duckling had no idea where he was!

What was that noise? A big hunting dog was right there scouting out the area! The ugly duckling tried to make himself as small as possible. He was so afraid to move that he stayed in the water all night.

When morning came, the ugly duckling was sure the dog had gone away. The baby duck was still lost, and now he was hungry, too. He was also a little bit scared. The duckling knew he needed to do something.

"I'll just have to try to find something to eat," said the ugly duckling. He hopped out of the pond and looked around. There was a farm down the road. He waddled closer to take a look. Near the farmhouse he saw a woman. "Peep," said the duckling.

The woman said, "You look hungry. Come get something to eat." When they got inside the house, the ugly duckling saw a cat and a pet hen. The cat and hen stared right at the ugly duckling. The duckling stared at the floor.

The duckling couldn't lay eggs like the hen or purr like the cat. They picked on him because he was different. After a few days, the duckling remembered how much he liked to be in the fresh air and how much he missed swimming in the water. One night he quietly left the house.

The duckling waddled farther down the road and soon found a lake where other wild ducks lived. In this lake the duckling could dive to the bottom and pop back up again to float. All the swimming helped him to grow bigger and stronger. Still, none of the wild ducks who lived there would even talk to him because they thought he was too ugly.

Soon the seasons changed. It was fall now. The leaves turned colors, and the air got cooler. The duckling found that the water was getting colder, too. One evening, just at sunset, a flock of beautiful birds flew overhead. Their feathers were shiny white, and they had long, graceful necks. The birds were flying south to find a warmer place to live for the winter.

The ugly duckling stretched his neck as far as he could to look at the beautiful birds. He felt sad as he watched them. Soon he was shivering, and he felt very lonely.

Winter came, and the pond turned to ice. A duck cannot swim on ice. The ugly duckling needed to practice, so he went in search of water that wasn't frozen.

Soon he came to a farmhouse. The fireplace had a roaring fire in it. Everything inside looked very warm and cozy. He waddled into the house and began his search. Finally he found something. It was much smaller than the pond, but it would just have to do. He jumped in and started to swim.

The farmer's wife heard a lot of splashing. She was very surprised to find a large bird inside the house! She quickly grabbed the broom and chased him back out into the snow, knocking over a fresh bucket of milk in the process. The children laughed and laughed at the big bird who had tried to swim in their bathtub.

The duckling was really scared now! He found a hiding place under some bushes. Snow fell all around him. He tried to stay warm.

The poor ugly duckling had a hard time that long winter. There was barely any food to eat, and the icy wind made him very cold. Just when he thought he couldn't stand it any more, something wonderful happened—spring arrived! Now there was warm sunshine and blooming flowers. Many birds came back from their winter homes.

It was now warm enough to go back on the lake. How good it felt to swim on the water again. He stretched his neck all around. When he looked down, what a surprise he got!

There in the water was the most beautiful bird he had ever seen. He looked at the swans swimming farther down the lake. They must know this swan below the water.

The ugly duckling was surprised when he heard someone speak to him. "Come join us," the swans said. What? Could this be true? Could the beautiful swans really be talking to him?

The ugly duckling looked down in the water again. Why, that wasn't another bird at all. It was his own reflection that he saw in the water. Over the winter, the ugly duckling had grown into a beautiful swan. He really wasn't a duck at all. No wonder he didn't fit in.

The other swans circled around him and stroked him with their beaks. All the young swan had gone through made him appreciate his newfound happiness. He saw beauty in all that surrounded him. He ruffled his feathers and thought, "I never dreamed I could be so happy when I was an ugly duckling."

One to Grow On

Patience

Most everyone was mean to the ugly duckling. They called him names and made fun of him. Do you think this made him feel good? Was it easy for him to be patient when this happened?

Sometimes it is hard to be patient with others who are different than us. Do you think things would be easier if everybody was the same?

Different people have different ways of seeing things. We can learn very important lessons by talking and listening to people who are different than we are. And remember, today's ugly duckling can be tomorrow's beautiful swan.

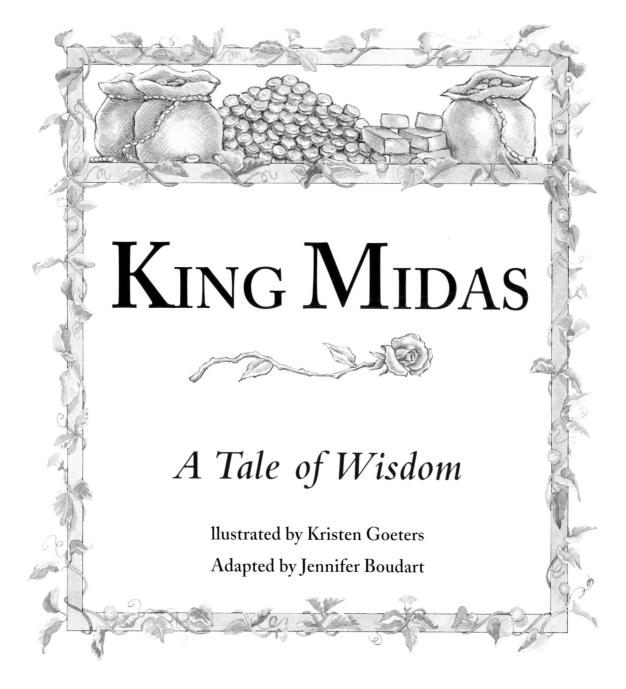

KING MIDAS

A Tale of Wisdom

Illustrated by Kristen Goeters

Adapted by Jennifer Boudart

There once was a king named Midas, who ruled a magical land of roses and sunshine. King Midas was rich beyond imagination, but he was also very selfish and foolish. He never enjoyed the warm sunshine or wonderful flowers of his beautiful kingdom. Instead King Midas liked to spend his days in a room in the basement of his castle where he kept his gold. Every day King Midas locked himself in the vault so he could count his money without anybody bothering him.

There was nothing that Midas would rather do than count his riches. His gold made him feel important, and he loved to surround himself with it. Each morning at the crack of dawn King Midas headed straight to the vault. He stayed with his gold until he went to sleep at night. And even then he dreamed of how to get more.

King Midas had a beautiful daughter named Marygold. She was very different from her father. Marygold did not pay any attention to gold, and she was not at all selfish. Marygold liked to spend her days outdoors. Day after day Marygold walked happily among the roses in the garden. It was her favorite place. She loved taking care of all the beautiful flowers and watering them so they would grow to be even taller than she was. There was nothing Marygold liked better than smelling the sweet scent of the roses and watching the pretty butterflies as they flew about.

Marygold was sorry that her father never joined her in the garden. She wished he would leave his gold and come outside to see what a lovely place she had created. She was certain that her father would really enjoy her flowers, especially the beautiful roses, if he ever saw them.

One day Midas was busy counting his gold in the vault when a mysterious stranger appeared. "How did you get in here?" asked King Midas.

"Well," said the stranger, "I have some magical powers. My, you certainly have a lot of gold."

"Yes," said Midas, "but I could always use more."

"I could give you the power to turn all that you touch into gold," said the stranger. "Would you like that?"

"Yes! Yes! Of course I would," Midas excitedly said to the mysterious stranger. "I would like that very much!"

"Very well," said the stranger. "After the next sunrise, anything you touch will turn to gold."

King Midas spent that night wide awake staring through a window in the castle. He could hardly wait for the sun to rise. When the dawn's light finally appeared, Midas reached to push away the curtain, and it turned into solid gold! Then Midas grabbed his chair, and it turned to gold, too! Midas grew very excited with his new magical power. He ran from room to room touching everything he could reach—tables, mirrors, candlesticks, paintings, and doors. Just like the mysterious stranger had promised, everything turned to gold.

Then King Midas rushed from his castle into Marygold's garden. He knew that this was his daughter's favorite place. Midas laid his hands on a rose, and it turned from scarlet red to gold. "How delighted Marygold will be," Midas said to himself, "when she finds I have turned all of her flowers into precious gold!"

Soon the king's stomach began to rumble. Changing things to gold had made him very hungry! Midas returned to the castle and ordered a delicious breakfast for himself.

Servants brought plates piled high with the freshest fruit, the warmest bread, and the tastiest cheese. Normally King Midas began eating breakfast with a yummy strawberry. Today he carefully chose the juiciest one. But as soon as he touched it, the strawberry changed to gold. Midas was hungry, but he could not eat! Then King Midas grabbed a goblet of water and raised it to his lips, but the water turned to gold, too!

Midas became dizzy with thirst and hunger. He wanted to eat some food very badly, but it all turned to gold when he touched it!

Suddenly Marygold came into the room. She held a gold rose and was crying.

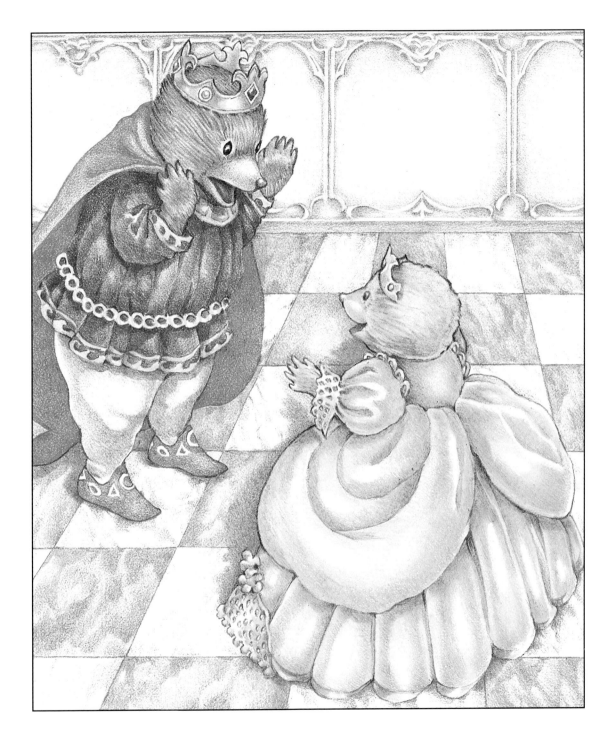

Marygold sat at the table with her father and sobbed. "Look at this poor rose," she cried. "How could this have happened?"

"I made it happen, Marygold," answered King Midas. "I thought you would like to see your flowers turned into beautiful and valuable pieces of gold."

"My roses are ruined!" exclaimed Marygold. "They no longer smell sweet, they no longer feel like velvet, and they no longer make the butterflies dance. The roses might be gold, but they are no longer valuable to me. They are worthless!"

Like all fathers, King Midas hated to see his daughter unhappy. He wanted to make Marygold feel better, and without thinking, he rushed over to to give her a comforting hug. As soon as King Midas touched her, Marygold turned into solid gold!

King Midas was shocked at what he had done to Marygold. He quickly ran from the golden statue that used to be his daughter. He now knew his wish to turn all that he touched to gold had been a curse, not a blessing. If only he could turn back time, then he could get his beautiful daughter back.

Just then the mysterious stranger returned and asked, "Aren't you pleased with all your gold?"

"I was very foolish," King Midas answered. "I don't care about gold anymore. I just want Marygold again. Please save my daughter, and you can have all of my gold."

"I do not want your gold, Midas. I just wanted to teach you a lesson. To get your daughter back, simply go to the river beyond the rose garden. Dive into its waters and bring back enough water to sprinkle over the things you have turned to gold. They will all return to normal."

At once King Midas called out to all the servants in the castle. "Gather every pail, bucket, bowl, and pitcher you can find," he shouted. "Then follow me to the river beyond the rose garden! I need your help to change Marygold and all the flowers back to normal." Without another word Midas and the servants ran to the river's edge.

Midas leaped into the cold, rushing water of the river, and it instantly began to turn golden yellow. Midas watched as the golden layer fell to the bottom of the river. Quickly King Midas and his servants filled all the pails and bowls with water and returned to the castle. King Midas went straight to the dining hall, and he splashed water over every golden object, just like the mysterious stranger had told him to do. When Midas saw Marygold change from gold back to her normal self, his heart filled with joy.

King Midas was very thankful and relieved to have his daughter back. Together he and Marygold went outside and changed all the gold flowers back to beautiful red roses. The mysterious stranger had taught Midas a valuable lesson: there are more important things in life than gold.

From that day on, King Midas was happier than he had ever been before. He no longer spent his days locked away in the vault all by himself. Instead King Midas shared time with Marygold in the garden. Now Midas loved spending time outdoors. He cared little for gold and riches, and he saw the true beauty of flowers, butterflies, and of his most valuable treasure, Marygold.

The only gold that King Midas cared for now was the golden sunshine.

One to Grow On

Wisdom

Wisdom is learning to make the right choices. This story shows us that it is not always easy to do the wise thing. King Midas loved gold and thought the more he had, the happier he would be.

A wise person knows that money or gold can't buy happiness and that simple things can be the best. In the end King Midas grew wiser. He found out that gold did not make him happy and that the best things in life—his daughter, flowers, and the warm sunshine—are free.

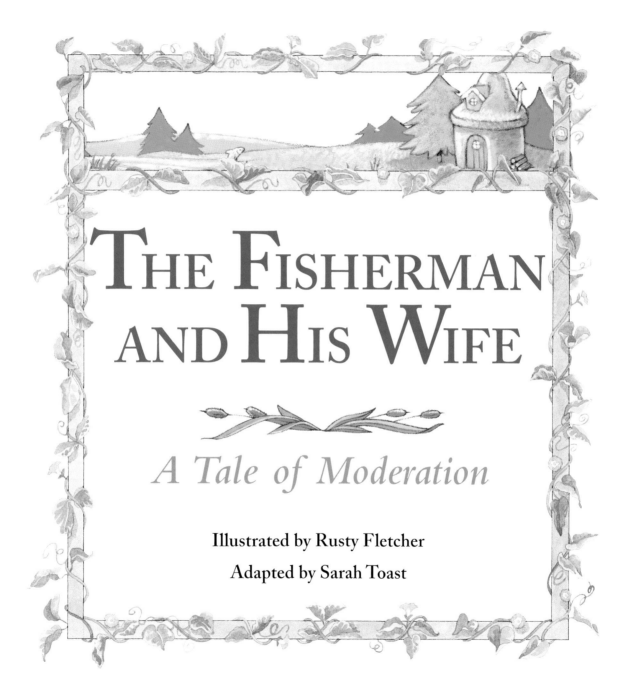

THE FISHERMAN AND HIS WIFE

A Tale of Moderation

Illustrated by Rusty Fletcher

Adapted by Sarah Toast

Once upon a time, a poor fisherman and his wife lived in a little cottage near a river. Every day the fisherman went to the river and fished for their dinner.

One day the fisherman caught a magical fish in his net. It said, "Fisherman, I beg you to let me live. I am not really a fish, I am an enchanted prince. Please let me swim away."

The fisherman quickly agreed to let the fish go. "Say no more," said the fisherman. "I am quite willing to set free a fish that can talk!"

"For that, I will grant you a wish," said the fish, but the fisherman said there was nothing he needed.

The fisherman let the fish go free. When he went home, his wife asked, "Husband, what have you caught for me to cook for our dinner?"

"I haven't brought anything home," he said. "I did catch a big fish. But he claimed to be an enchanted prince, so I threw him back into the water."

"Oh dear!" she said. "You might at least have made a wish before you set him free!"

"I couldn't think of anything that we needed," replied her husband. "What would you have wished for?"

"Well, we certainly could use a nicer place to live. I'm sure that if you go back and ask the fish for a nicer house, he will gladly give it to you!"

The fisherman did not really think that they needed a nicer house, but he did as his wife asked.

The fisherman went to the river and called:
Princely fish that I set free,
Hear my words and come to me.

Just as soon as the fisherman had finished reciting this rhyme, the fish appeared.

"Why did you call me?" the fish asked.

The fisherman was a little nervous, but he got up his nerve and answered, "My wife would like to make a wish after all."

"And what is her wish?" asked the fish.

"She doesn't want to live in a tiny cottage anymore," said the fisherman. "She would like to live in a nicer home."

"Go home to your wife," said the fish. "She already has her wish."

The fisherman hurried back home. There was his wife waving from the doorway of a pretty, new house.

The house was filled with everything they could possibly need. "Now we can be happy," the fisherman said.

But a few days later his wife said, "Husband, this house is too small. We need more space! Go back to the river and ask the fish for a castle!"

The fisherman wanted his wife to be happy, so he went back to the river and called:

>*Princely fish that I set free,*
>*Hear my words and come to me.*

Again, just as soon as the fisherman finished speaking, the fish appeared. "Now what?" asked the fish.

The fisherman thought the fish sounded just a tiny bit angry. "Alas, I must ask another favor of you," the fisherman said regretfully. "It seems as though my wife now wants to live in a castle."

"Go home. She is already there," said the fish.

When the fisherman returned home, his wife waved to him from the balcony of a huge castle. Its rooms were full of golden furniture, and the tables were overflowing with wonderful things to eat.

"Isn't everything beautiful?" asked the wife. The fisherman nodded his head in agreement. He looked at all the things inside the magnificent castle. The fisherman thought that now they must have everything they could ever possibly want.

But early the next morning the wife woke up frowning. She said, "Husband, we live in a castle. It is only right that we should be king and queen of all the land."

The fisherman really didn't want to be king, but his wife insisted. The unhappy fisherman finally gave in and went back to the river.

Once again the fisherman approached the spot where he had met the enchanted fish. And once again he called out:

Princely fish that I set free,
Hear my words and come to me.

The fish appeared as before. This time, though, the river and the sky seemed to get darker. "What is it now?" he asked.

The fisherman was sure the fish was unhappy, but he asked his favor anyway. "I'm afraid my wife wants us to be king and queen," sighed the fisherman.

"Go home. She is already queen," said the fish.

Sure enough, when the fisherman arrived back at the castle, his wife was sitting on a high, gold throne. "Now that you are queen," said the fisherman, "surely you will not wish for anything more."

"I'm not at all sure of that," said the queen. "I have a feeling there is something else we need."

That night the fisherman slept well. His wife, however, lay awake tossing and turning. She was busy wondering what her next wish would be.

Just as the wife was about to fall asleep, the morning sun came up. Bright sunlight poured in through the royal bedroom window. The wife sat up in bed.

"Husband!" she called out. "I do not think the sun should be allowed to rise without my permission! You go tell that enchanted fish of yours that I want to have complete power over the rising and setting of the sun!"

"Wife," said the fisherman, "please don't make me go back and call the fish again. I fear that this time the favor is too much to ask!"

At this, the wife flew into a rage. "Go tell the fish to grant my wish!" she shouted.

Quaking with fear, the fisherman got dressed. He hurried out of the castle and headed toward the river. As he walked, strong winds began to blow, and the river began to rage.

The fisherman stumbled to the riverbank. The wind was so strong that he could barely hear his own voice. As he stood facing out over the water he called:

Princely fish that I set free,
Hear my words and come to me.

A bright bolt of lightning struck the river's edge, and a loud clap of thunder rang through the air. "What does your wife want now?" bellowed the fish as he rose up through the choppy waves.

"Oh fish," said the fisherman fearfully, "she wants the power to make the sun rise and set."

"Go home to your wife," said the fish.

Suddenly the wind stopped blowing just as quickly as it had started. The waves in the river calmed, and the water was peaceful again. The fisherman went home to find his wife in front of their humble cottage.

"Husband," said the wife, "I am so sorry that I got carried away with greed. Each new and better thing only made me think I wanted more. But the more I got, the more unhappy I became. I forgot to be happy with what I already had."

"It's my fault, too," the fisherman said. "When you wanted more, I asked the fish for it."

The fisherman lovingly kissed his wife, took his net, and went to the river. He gazed into the clear blue water as he fished.

That night he brought his wife a nice, plain fish for their dinner.

One to Grow On

Moderation

The fisherman and his wife learned a great deal about moderation. Moderation means not having too much or too little of anything. Instead of being thankful for what she had, the fisherman's wife always wanted more.

Have you ever had too much of something? Like the fisherman and his wife, maybe you have learned that less can be better. Sometimes simple things can make us happier than all the castles and crowns in the world.

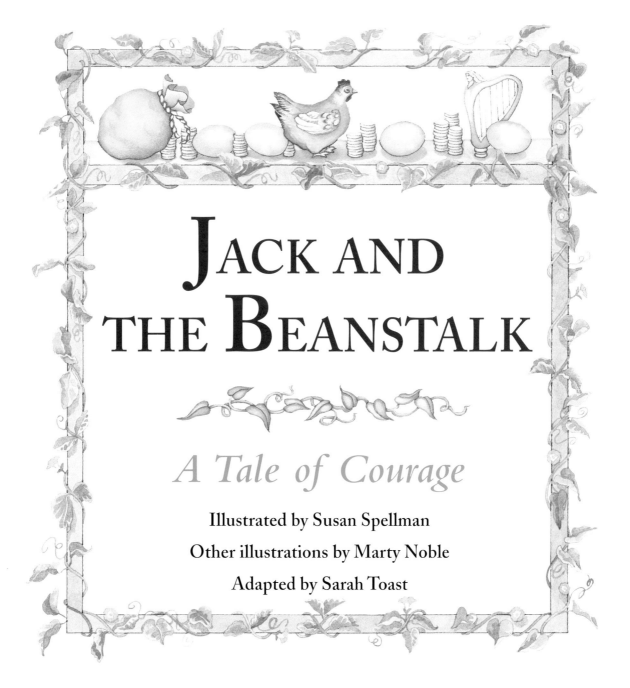

JACK AND THE BEANSTALK

A Tale of Courage

Illustrated by Susan Spellman

Other illustrations by Marty Noble

Adapted by Sarah Toast

A poor woman lived out in the country with her son, Jack. Years ago, when Jack was just a baby, a terrible giant had done away with Jack's father and had stolen his gold and treasure. The woman was left to raise Jack as best she could.

Jack and his mother both worked hard. But no matter how hard they tried, there never seemed to be enough money to keep food on the table. At last there was no money left at all. Jack's mother said, "Jack, dear, take the cow to market today, and sell her for a good price."

On his way to market, Jack met a stranger. The man asked where he was going. Jack replied, "I'm going to market to sell this cow, so my mother and I can have food to eat."

"I will give you these five magic beans for the cow," said the stranger. Jack thought that was a good deal, so he traded his cow for five magic beans.

When Jack returned to the cottage, he burst through the door and said, "Look at the five magic beans I got for the cow!"

"Jack, what have you done? Those beans aren't worth anything! Now we will go hungry," cried his mother as she threw the beans out the window. Jack and his mother quietly went to bed without any supper.

Jack woke up early the next morning and went outside. He was amazed to see a huge beanstalk had sprung up outside the window during the night. It had grown so high that he couldn't see the top. Although he was afraid of the long, hard climb, Jack decided to see where it led. Maybe he could find a way to help his mother.

Jack climbed the beanstalk for a very long time. When he finally reached the top, he saw a great castle.

Tired and hungry after his long climb, Jack set out for the castle to ask for something to eat and some work to do. When he reached the castle steps, he saw a woman ten times larger than anyone he had ever seen. "Please, ma'am," said Jack, "I haven't eaten for a very long time. Could you give me supper?"

"If you stay here, you'll be the giant's supper," the woman said. Jack was scared. He realized that this was the wife of the giant—the same giant who had killed his father. However, he was so hungry that he still begged to eat there. The woman finally gave in and let Jack come into the kitchen. She fixed a plate of food and gave it to him.

Jack had just finished eating when he heard the thump, thump, thump of heavy footsteps. Jack was so frightened he couldn't move. Just as the giant came into the kitchen, the woman popped Jack into the cool oven to hide him.

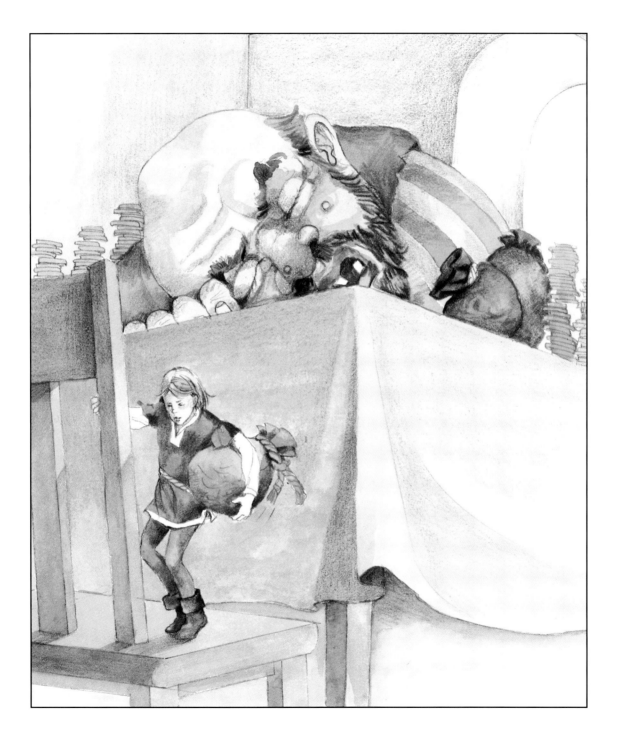

When the giant arrived, he sniffed the air and roared:

Fee-fi-fo-fum!
I smell the blood of an Englishman!

"It's just your supper that you smell," said the giant's wife.

The giant gobbled up his entire supper. Jack watched from his hiding place. He had never seen anyone eat so much food. Then the giant said to his wife, "Bring me my gold!"

The woman brought out the gold. Jack kept very still as he watched the giant count the gold over and over. Finally the giant fell asleep. Jack's mother once told him that his father's gold had been stolen by the mean giant. Jack quietly climbed up on the table. Then he snatched a bag of gold and ran away.

When Jack reached the beanstalk, he dropped the gold down to his mother's garden and then climbed down as fast as he could.

Jack's mother was very happy when the gold coins rained down and Jack came back safely. The mother and son made the gold last for a very long time, but finally there was no more. Jack decided to climb the beanstalk again. He would have to get back all of his father's treasure despite any danger.

Jack returned to the giant's castle. He crept softly into the kitchen and hid in the oven again. Soon the giant's footsteps shook the floor, and he roared:

Fee-fi-fo-fum!
I smell the blood of an Englishman!

"There's no one here," said the giant's wife. The giant ate his supper quickly, then bellowed for his hen.

Then the giant shouted, "Lay!" Jack peeked out and saw the hen lay a perfect golden egg. After the giant fell asleep, Jack jumped out of the oven, grabbed the hen, and ran away.

When Jack reached the beanstalk, he scaled down quickly while carrying the hen. Jack's mother told him that this hen also had belonged to his father, and so had a magic harp.

The hen laid a golden egg every time it was told to lay, so Jack and his mother now had everything they needed. After awhile, however, Jack thought about the harp that used to belong to his father. Even though he would face great danger, Jack decided to climb the beanstalk one last time. He would make his way to the castle and find the harp.

As soon as he arrived at the castle, Jack sneaked into the kitchen and hid in a huge copper pot. The giant thumped into the kitchen at suppertime, sniffing the air:

Fee-fi-fo-fum!

This time the giant's wife scurried over to the oven and looked inside, but it was empty.

The giant looked all around the kitchen. Jack was terribly afraid of being found. Luckily the giant didn't check inside the big pots, so he didn't find Jack.

The giant gobbled his supper and then called for his harp. His wife brought in a very special harp made of gold. The giant commanded the harp to play. Its golden strings played beautiful music. Then the harp began to sing a lullaby.

Soon the giant fell asleep. When Jack heard snoring, he climbed out of the pot and onto the table. For a moment, he was afraid to be so near to the giant. He took a deep breath, grabbed the harp, and started to run off with it.

"Master! Master!" the harp cried. The giant awoke with a start and made a grab for Jack. With the harp in his arms, Jack jumped off the table and ran for his life.

Jack could hear the giant's thunderous footsteps crashing down right behind him. The giant took very big steps, but he had eaten a huge supper. All that food slowed him down just enough, and Jack was able to reach the beanstalk first.

Jack hurried down the beanstalk with the harp. He called to his mother as he went, "Mother! Bring me the ax!" The giant was already halfway down the beanstalk when Jack reached the ground. Jack quickly took the ax from his mother and with one mighty chop, he cut down the beanstalk. The giant crashed down to the ground, and that was the end of him!

Brave Jack and his mother lived happily ever after.

Courage

Jack was courageous when he climbed the beanstalk. He knew it would be a very difficult task, and he did not know what he might find at the top. He was brave when he took it upon himself to get back his father's gold, especially since the danger was great. Having courage means overcoming fear in order to help yourself or others.

Sometimes it is very difficult to be courageous. Other times people act courageously almost without thinking. Can you think of someone who has shown courage? How did they show their bravery?

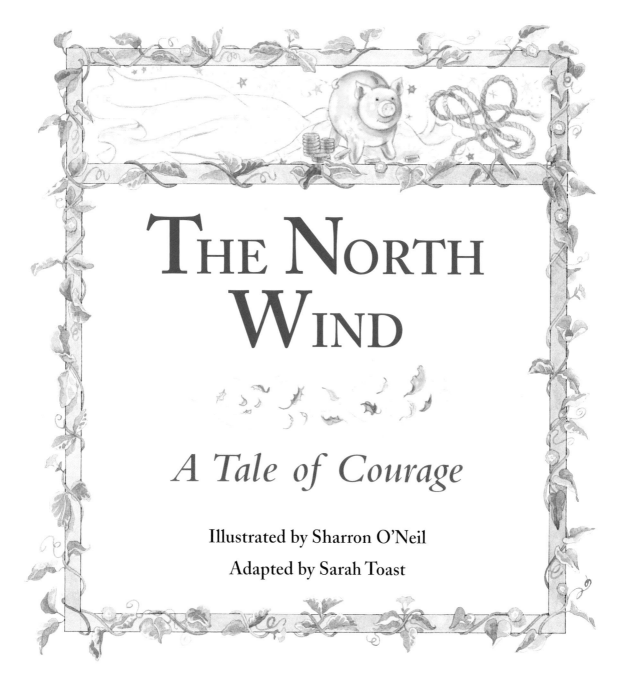

THE NORTH WIND

A Tale of Courage

Illustrated by Sharron O'Neil

Adapted by Sarah Toast

Long ago in a northern land, a little boy lived with his mother. One day the boy's mother sent him into town to buy some oats. She wanted to make warm oatmeal for breakfast and good oatmeal bread for the rest of the day.

The boy went to the mill and bought the oats. Then he walked back home, taking care not to spill the oats from his basket. But as the boy walked home, the cold North Wind swept down upon him. With one great windy puff, the North Wind blew away all of the boy's oats, scattering them throughout the village.

The boy turned around and walked back to the mill. There he had his basket filled with oats again. As he walked home, the North Wind again swirled around the boy and scattered the oats with one puff. After this happened a third time, the little boy had no money left to buy oats.

The boy was sad when he got home and told his mother what had happened. He made up his mind that he would visit the North Wind and try to get the oats back.

It was a long, long walk through the northern woods to where the North Wind lived. As he trudged along, it grew colder and colder, and the boy grew very afraid. By the time he reached the North Wind's door, his hand was shaking so hard that it knocked on the door all by itself.

The gruff North Wind came to the door. "What is it you want?" he asked in his growly voice.

The boy was afraid of the grumpy North Wind, but he gathered up his courage. "I have come to ask you to give back our oats," he said. "My mother and I do not have much to eat, and now our money is gone as well."

"I can't give back your oats," said the North Wind. "They have been scattered to the winds. But you and your mother are poor, and you were brave to come here. For this, I will give you a magic tablecloth."

The North Wind told the boy to lay the cloth on the table and say "Cloth, cloth! Serve up food!" The cloth would make all the food that he and his mother could eat. The boy was very pleased with the gift. He thanked the North Wind as he set off for home with the cloth.

When it began to get dark, the boy decided to spend the night at an inn. He laid the cloth on a table in the dining room and said, "Cloth, cloth! Serve up food!" The innkeeper was amazed to see all the delicious food appear. He wanted to keep the tablecloth for himself.

After the boy fell asleep, the innkeeper crept up the stairs carrying an ordinary tablecloth that looked just like the boy's magical one. He entered the boy's room and traded the magical cloth for the plain one.

In the morning the boy took the cloth and walked the rest of the way home. When he told his mother the North Wind had given them a magic cloth, she said, "Seeing is believing. Show me what the cloth does."

The boy proudly laid the cloth on their little kitchen table and said, "Cloth, cloth! Serve up food!" Nothing happened. Not even a crust of bread appeared on the table, no matter how many times the boy said the magic words. He and his mother went hungry that day.

The next morning the boy made up his mind to go back to the North Wind and tell him that the cloth didn't work.

It was a long walk back to the home of the North Wind. By the time the boy knocked on the door, he was very tired and a little bit scared to complain about the magic cloth.

The North Wind opened the door and said, "Hello again. What do you want?"

"I've come to tell you that you took our oatmeal, and the cloth you gave us doesn't serve food." The boy shivered a little as he spoke.

"I don't have another magic cloth, and I don't have any oats," said the North Wind. "But I do have a piggy bank that I can give you. If you say, 'Piggy bank, make money!' it will give you all the money you need."

The boy thanked the North Wind and started home with a smile. It was already late when he reached the inn, so he decided to stop there again.

When the time came to pay for his dinner at the inn, the boy set the piggy bank on the table and said, "Piggy bank, make money!" Then he reached into the piggy bank and pulled out enough coins to pay the innkeeper for dinner and a room for the night.

After dinner the boy went right upstairs to bed. He was sound asleep when the innkeeper crept into the room with an ordinary piggy bank under his arm. He took the boy's magic piggy bank and left the ordinary one in its place.

The next morning when the boy reached home, he happily told his mother that the North Wind had given them a magic piggy bank. "I'll believe it when I see it work," said his mother. When the boy said "Piggy bank, make money!" not one coin came out of the bank.

The boy and his mother had no food left and no money. The boy was afraid to visit the grumpy North Wind again, but he knew he had to get help.

Once more the boy set out on the long walk to the home of the North Wind. This time the North Wind was angrier than ever. He wanted the boy to stop bothering him, and the North Wind opened the door before the boy even knocked.

"Well, what do you want now?" roared the North Wind with his icy breath.

"I must get my oats back," said the boy. "The piggy bank doesn't work."

"I have only one thing left," said the North Wind. "It is a magic rope that will tie someone up if you say 'Rope, rope! Tie him up!' Because you have come all this way, I will give it to you."

The boy thanked the North Wind and set out for home again. By now he figured out what had happened to his magic cloth and his piggy bank, so he had an idea what to do with the magic rope.

When he reached the inn on the way home, the boy again stopped for the night. Although he didn't have any money, the innkeeper gave him dinner and a place to sleep. The innkeeper thought the rope the boy was carrying might be magic, and he planned to steal it. After dinner the boy went right upstairs to bed, but this time he only pretended to go to sleep.

Later the innkeeper crept into the boy's room to replace the magical rope with ordinary rope. When he came close to the boy's bed, the boy sprang up and shouted, "Rope, rope! Tie him up!" The magic rope wrapped itself many times around the innkeeper and tied him up.

The innkeeper struggled but could not get loose. The boy said, "I won't untie you until you give me back my magic cloth and magic piggy bank!" The innkeeper struggled some more, but at last he said, "Take them back! Just set me free!" The boy kindly let the innkeeper go.

With his magical things in hand, the boy returned home. This time he was able to show his mother the magic items. The cloth provided them with plenty of food, and the piggy bank gave them money to meet their needs. In case they ever needed its help, the rope was nearby to protect them.

The boy went to see the North Wind one last time — to thank him for his help. This time he was not afraid at all.

One to Grow On

Courage

Courage means doing the right thing even when you are scared. The boy in this story offers some good examples of courage. Despite being scared, the boy visited the frightening North Wind because he wanted to help his mother and he knew it was the right thing to do. Fortunately the North Wind respected the boy's courage and helped as much as he could.

The boy learned an important lesson: sometimes we are afraid when there is really no reason to be. In the end the boy dealt bravely with the innkeeper who had stolen his things. Because of the boy's bravery and persistence, he and his mother lived happily ever after.

THE TORTOISE AND THE HARE

A Tale of Perseverance

Illustrated by Krista Brauckmann-Towns

Other illustrations by Marty Noble

Adapted by Mary Rowitz

One day a fast hare hopped into the path of a slow tortoise. "It must be awful to be so slow," said the hare. "Fast is the only way to go."

The tortoise slowly shook his head. "Fast is your style, but slow and steady gets me where I want to go."

"As long as you are in no hurry," said the hare. "If you were ever in a race, you would surely lose."

The tortoise shook his head again. "Don't be so sure. I have won a few races. Perhaps I could win another today."

"Are you saying you want to race me?" asked the hare.

The tortoise nodded as quickly as he could, which was not very quick at all.

"Okay then, let's race," said the hare. "But you'll never win."

"We'll see," the tortoise said. "Slow and steady wins the race."

News of the race spread quickly. Friends of the tortoise and the hare gathered to watch.

"Race along the dirt path," said the fox. Then he waved a red flag to start the race. They were off.

The hare sprinted off to a very fast start. He was so far ahead that when he looked back, he couldn't see the tortoise anymore. The hare stopped running.

The tired hare decided to take a short nap alongside the road. "I could sleep for hours and that slowpoke still would not catch up to me," the hare said. "And even if he did, I surely would wake up as he walked by."

The hare fell fast asleep along the side of the racecourse. Hours later, the tortoise finally caught up with him! As he got closer to the sleeping hare, the tortoise could hear his snoring. He seemed to be in a very deep sleep, but the tortoise didn't want to take any chances. Very carefully the tortoise walked past the hare on his tiptoes. He moved extra slowly and extra quietly so he would not wake up the hare as he walked by.

The tortoise smiled with pride when he passed the hare. "Slow and steady wins the race," he whispered as he headed toward the finish line. "Slow and steady wins the race."

As the tortoise looked down the dirt path, he could see everyone gathered at the finish line. The tortoise could hardly wait to see their looks when he crossed the line first.

When the hare finally woke up, he saw a trail of tortoise prints. He leaped to his feet and looked ahead to the finish line. The tortoise was just about to win the race!

The hare ran down the path as fast as he could, but it was too late. The slow and steady tortoise had already won!

The tortoise looked very pleased with himself. It was not every day that he beat a fast hare in a race.

The hare felt foolish that he had lost to the tortoise, and he was very tired from running so fast at the end of the race. He fell to the ground to catch his breath.

The fox let out a long whistle. "Tell me," he said to the tortoise, "how did you beat the fast hare?"

"It's like I always said, slow and steady wins the race."

One to Grow On

Perseverance

Perseverance means never giving up. Early in the race, it would have been easy for the tortoise to quit — the hare was winning by so much that it looked like the tortoise could never catch up. Even though everyone laughed at the tortoise and no one thought he had a chance of winning, he kept going. The tortoise showed the other animals that anything is possible with a little perseverance.

As you grow, you will learn that things don't always come easily. Sometimes we have to work a little harder to be good at something. But as the tortoise shows us, wonderful things can happen when you don't give up.